PAWS FOR ALARM

Book 2 in the Canine Confections Mystery series

Amy Hueston

CHAPTER ONE

"My head feels wonky," Jenny said from her side of Patisserie of Palm Beach's patio table.

"Another headache?" I asked.

The manager of the pastry shop two doors down from Canine Confections seemed to be complaining a lot about headaches lately. I was beginning to worry.

She dismissed my question, swiveled her head up and down ritzy Worth Avenue and blinked at the morning light. "So, Samantha Armstrong," she said. "Here you are, here I am, and here is Sweet Pea ..." She leaned down and scruffed my dog's fuzzy ears. "Where's everybody else?"

"No idea."

For the past month, a few of our fellow shopkeepers had been meeting for a good old-fashioned coffee klatch on the patio of the pastry shop.

By this time of the morning, we were normally knocking back cappuccinos and discussing our latest marketing ideas or dating disasters.

Sweet Pea tilted her head so Jenny could reach the exact right spot behind her folded Labrador mix ears and licked her hand.

"She sure is affectionate," Jenny said.

"As long as you don't murder anybody."

Jenny's jaw dropped.

"That was blunt," I said and chuckled awkwardly. "I only meant the one person she never licked was the woman who killed Whitney." Whitney, the former owner of Patisserie—and of Sweet Pea—whom I had found dead on Canine Confections' floor a month ago. I had read that a flippant attitude was a way for the mind to digest awful things until it's ready to deal, but geez, my coldness sounded crass.

Jenny eyed me with suspicion but tucked a loose, sun-bleached strand of hair behind her ear and immediately turned her attention to the four empty chairs at the patio table. "So much for coffee klatch today."

"No!" I said with more feeling than the situation warranted.

Jenny raised her eyebrows.

Our coffee klatch had become a cozy gathering, something to count on. After all I had been through—moving to a new town where I felt as out of place as a dinosaur in a china shop, opening a dog bakery with what turned out to be my Aunt Mary's life savings, finding a dead body on the morning of my grand opening, and trying to drum up consistent business for the dog bakery everyone in Palm Beach thought of as a murder site—I wasn't ready to let go of my morning ritual with my new circle of friends.

"They'll show," I said firmly.

As if on cue, Dominique, the Palm Beach socialite who doesn't *work* on Worth Avenue but jogs on it like clockwork every morning, exited Patisserie's front door and plopped a pumpkin on the table.

"Happy Halloween to you, too," I said with a laugh and sipped my cappuccino.

Sweet Pea jumped up, kissed Dominique's calf one time, then returned to her spot next to me.

Jenny asked, "Doesn't taking the shortcut through the back door of Patisserie sort of defeat the purpose of getting your morning exercise?"

"I was on my way to my car parked back there when I saw Frederika's pumpkin display in front of her flower shop." Dominique shrugged one toned shoulder. "I couldn't resist buying one, but I didn't feel like lugging it around the building."

"You were going to miss coffee klatch?" Jenny asked.

Dominique nodded and winced as she pressed in on her 200-sit-ups-a-day abdomen with a hand that, by the look of the blisters, held a tennis racket a little too overzealously.

I laughed at the oversized gourd as large as a beach ball. "Is it big enough?"

"I thought one of you might want to use it for your bakeries. Make some pumpkin pie or something."

Jenny said, "Samantha owns a dog bakery. This is a pastry shop and it's for humans."

"Excuse me, Miss Semantics," Dominique replied.

Jenny said excitedly, "I think we should make a jack-o-lantern with it." She looked at me to get my take on the idea, then held a hand to her forehead and grimaced.

"Do whatever you want, I bought it to cheer myself up." Dominique pressed her hands into her stomach. "My stomach has been killing me. I must have eaten some bad sushi or something last night." She touched her fingers to her clavicle. "Plus, I lost my necklace during my jog."

"The one your grandmother gave you?" Jenny asked.

"The clasp was loose. I checked to make sure it was on while I jogged past Jimmy Choo, and when I felt for it in front of Starbucks, it was gone."

I licked the foamy cinnamon on my lips and started to jump up from my chair. "So let's go check the sidewalk between Jimmy Choo and Starbucks."

Dominique shook her head and drank from her water bottle. "I went back to check as soon as it started to get light out. It's not there."

I sat back down. "It would be funny if whoever picked it up is the same person who is stealing from the shops around here."

"Hilarious," Jenny responded.

Dominique twisted the cap of her water bottle back and forth like it was the thief's neck instead of an innocent plastic thingamabob. "One of these days, I'm going to find out who it is and have a little chat with them." The muscles in her biceps shifted with each twist of the cap.

"You keep saying that," Jenny said with a small smile.

"And I mean it."

Jenny and I exchanged nervous glances.

Dominique tilted the remains of her water bottle into her mouth with blistered fingers. "There's one person I see window-shopping every morning but I can't make out who it is. Medium-height, and they wear a coat, hat, and gloves, so I don't know who it is or what they're doing. They can't be jogging or walking with that get-up on. I called out to them yesterday and yelled that I'd find out who they were."

I set my cappuccino down on the saucer. "They're trying to be incognito? You think it's the thief?"

Dominique pressed her hands to her stomach again and sat down. "Who else?"

"You should tell the police," I said.

"Tell them what? 'Hey Officer, I see someone walking around in a coat at four a.m., and it might be the same person who is stealing from the shops.' I can see how that would go over."

"You can tell them you see someone strange walking around in a coat," I offered.

"They probably have better things to do than worry about another eccentric person in Palm Beach." Dominique slowly stood up while Jenny and I eyed her with concern. "The next time I see that weirdo in a coat lurking about, I'll knock them out before they know what hit them."

Dominique left us with the pumpkin as she re-entered Patisserie from the front to leave out the back.

Jenny picked up the monstrous orange gourd. "You okay if I take this and make a jack-o-lantern?"

"Sure, but won't it be rotten by the time Halloween comes next week?"

"Don't they sell something to prevent pumpkins from rotting so fast?"

"Don't ask me. The only thing I know about arts and crafts is that I can make an outline of a turkey by tracing my hand."

Jenny heaved the pumpkin up in her arms and headed to the front door of the pastry shop. "I guess everyone else is a no-show."

Sweet Pea instantly jumped to her feet when I stood up.

"Guess so. See you later, alligator," I said to Jenny and left with Sweet Pea.

My dog and I strolled two shops down to Canine Confections. "Why did Tracy miss coffee klatch?"

She stared up at me and lolled her tongue.

I tried to insert my key into the front door of Confections but the door opened an inch. It was not only *not* locked, but not even shut.

"We haven't been here yet this morning," I said to Sweet Pea. "I know I asked Tracy to lock up last night on our way out. Think she forgot?"

Sweet Pea tentatively wagged her tail at my questioning tone.

I froze when a hand pressed on my left shoulder from behind, then whirled around breathlessly, feeling like a ghost had floated over my grave.

"Geez!" I shouted at Tracy, giggling in front of me. "What are you, twelve years old?" I smiled in spite of myself.

"Nope," she answered. "Twenty-seven, like you."

"You'd never know it," I grumbled. "Surprises like that are what I *don't* need during the spookiest time of the year."

Sweet Pea waved her tail from side to side and licked Tracy's hands in greeting.

I swung Confections' door wide …

… and my jaw dropped at the second surprise of the day.

CHAPTER TWO

C anine Confections stood in shambles—chairs overturned, fancy napkin holders toppled, turquoise chair cushions thrown on the floor, my current crossword puzzle magazine tossed to the side. Tears burned my eyes. I handed Sweet Pea's leash to Tracy to hold onto from a safe distance, then tiptoed over to the display case. The last time somebody broke into my dog bakery, I found dead Whitney Goodwin on the floor.

I peeked around the counter with half-closed eyes and ...

... found nothing but the bare tile floor. *Thank God.*

"Let's get out of here," I said to Tracy and Sweet Pea as I led the way to the front door in case the intruder ran from the back room.

Huddled on the sidewalk under Canine Confections' pink canopy, I called 911 from my cell while Tracy allowed enough lead on Sweet Pea's leash for her to sniff one of the two palm trees that bracketed the dog bakery. A couple of early risers strolled past in the South Florida costume of lime green and pastel pink.

I slipped my cell back into the pocket of my linen trousers and reached for Sweet Pea's leash. "We forgot to lock the front door last night."

Tracy's face turned the familiar shade of pink that I had seen from time to time ever since we met a month ago. "You mean me. *I* forgot." She tugged at her lip with her thumb and forefinger, a pained expression on her face.

"Relax, Trace," I said. "Everybody forgets to do stuff."

"I was here earlier today."

"You mean you *didn't* forget to lock the front door last night?"

"Yeah, I did."

I frowned at her, puzzled.

She explained, "I didn't come through the front door this morning. I came in through the back to practice making whipped cream with a teensy bit of peanut butter with the commercial mixer." Tracy directed her attention to Sweet Pea and petted the top of my furry girl's head.

"Then why did you come up from behind me at the front door?"

"I wanted you to be surprised when you opened the refrigerator and saw the whipped cream." Massaging Sweet Pea with both hands, she gestured with her chin to the narrow space between Confections and Bethany's art gallery next door. "I waited in the alley until you passed, and pretended I was just arriving for the day. The goal was that you would find the cream in the refrigerator as if Santa's elves were here during the night."

"Santa's elves aren't due to arrive for another two months," I said irritably and gazed through the large display window of Confections upon my poor café that looked like a tractor had plowed through. I stared past the overturned chairs at the door that separated the café from the back room. In my mind's eye, the intruder swung the door open and ran out to us on the sidewalk, then strangled us while the posh passersby looked on in their silk trousers.

I shook my head back to the present. "Just to be clear, you didn't come through the front door this morning? The door was unlocked all night?"

"Sorry." Her face fell.

Maybe I accorded too much responsibility to the young woman who, until a month ago, worked as a tabloid reporter.

"It's okay. No damage done." I glanced at the mess inside. "Or, you know, not *much* damage."

Tracy's gaze dropped to Sweet Pea sniffing the heels of another early morning Worth Avenue shopper sauntering past, this one in a pink sundress with green palm fronds, not unlike the bench cushions inside Confections. The shopper smiled politely and peered over her shoulder at the police car pulling up in front of Confections, then continued in the direction of Bethany's Gallery Bebe.

Bethany, elegant as ever in her sleek hairstyle and sophisticated heels, shook her head at the police car and shot me a dirty look, like it was my fault the police were at my dog bakery again. I turned my attention away from her and toward the officer striding over to me, Tracy, and Sweet Pea under the canopy.

The officer listened to us tell him everything that had happened thus far that morning—Tracy forgetting to lock the door last night and arriving early, and me inserting my key into an unlocked door this morning—and told us to wait while he checked inside Confections.

My stomach turned at what the officer might find, so I directed my attention to something sweet and fluffy. "You left a bowl of whipped cream in the walk-in refrigerator?"

Tracy, normally never without a ponytail and a smile, blew a piece of hair out of her eyes in frustration. "Yeah, but I couldn't get the whipped cream to fluff the way you do."

"Did you add a tiny bit of cornstarch or powdered sugar?"

"I thought you said to add flour!"

I chewed the inside of my mouth. Tracy wasn't much help in the baking department, but her eye for design was excellent.

"Trace," I said. "Remember we dropped the ball on ordering flour, and we only had enough left for the Peanut Butter Drops this morning?"

"You mean *I* dropped the ball."

Worth Avenue began to wake up and interrupted our conversation. A delivery truck wheeled past at a respectable twenty miles per hour. A shopper strolled by the still-closed Mystic Dreams across the street. Rick, the owner of Sophisticated Pet two shops to the left of Canine Confections, sauntered up to his shop. My stomach twitched a little at Sexy Stubble, not for the first time and probably not for the last.

The police officer exited the front of Confections. "You said you didn't notice anything missing?"

"It's hard to say with the mess in there, but it doesn't look like it." I turned to Tracy. "What do you think?"

"Like you said, it's hard to tell with everything thrown all over the place."

The officer wrote something in his notepad and slapped it shut. "That about does it. I just need you to sign the report."

"What about fingerprints?" I asked.

"If nothing is missing, it's only criminal mischief."

He made it sound like a couple of kids scooped an extra spoonful of ice cream from their parents' freezer.

"Isn't it at least breaking and entering?"

"Would it make you feel better if I labeled it like that for you?" he asked, all smart-mouth-like. "Bottom line, there isn't anything we can do if nothing was stolen."

"But this is my place of business," I said. "I can't have more trouble here after what happened."

"It's not like you found a dead body on the floor again," Tracy said to me. She looked at the officer. "Right?"

He met her gaze and shook his head that no, no he didn't find a dead body.

I signed the report and the officer left.

"Well, that was fun," I said and started to lead the charge back inside.

But as I stepped into the café, I heard a scream from the direction of Gallery Bebe and Patisserie. I raced back out of Confections' front door, Tracy and Sweet Pea at my heels. Across the street, Angelina from Mystic Dreams flew out of her shop. Up ahead, Bethany ran out the front door of her art gallery.

Another piercing scream rang from Patisserie. We jogged past Bebe to the patio where I had been with Jenny and Sweet Pea less than an hour ago. Bethany, ahead of us by twenty seconds, hesitated at Patisserie's front door.

"Suppose the intruder is still there?" she asked.

I handed Sweet Pea's leash to Tracy and nudged my way past Bethany. "Jenny might need help."

As we looked at each other for a moment, Angelina came gliding up in her usual garb of long skirt and gloves.

I sucked in a deep breath and listened for sounds from inside the pastry shop. *Nothing.* I stepped up to the door.

Tracy grabbed my arm. "You could get hurt."

A jagged crying sounded from inside. Someone needed our help.

"Stay out here with Sweet Pea," I said to Tracy.

With Angelina and Bethany at my heels, I slowly opened Patisserie's front door. The large pumpkin Dominique had bought sat on top of the display case.

And on the floor in front of the display case ...

Dominique lay sprawled with a knife in her chest.

CHAPTER THREE

Jenny stood sobbing over Dominique. Flour covered the fruit bowls and tray of napoleons on the counter. The stab wound produced more blood than I had found on Whitney from her blow to the head with my rolling pin.

"Oh my God," I whispered. I kneeled down to see if there were signs of life and found none.

Behind me, Bethany and Angelina drew in ragged breaths.

Dominique's head twisted garishly, and in addition to her blistered fingers, her lips were swollen. Tennis wouldn't explain that.

An empty petty-cash box lay open on the counter, along with a spilled bag of flour.

Jenny couldn't seem to contain her sobs. "I came out from beating a big batch of batter in the back and found her like this. The mixer must have made so much noise, I didn't even hear anything." She hiccupped. "It must have been the thief who's been breaking into all of the shops around here. He probably came in to steal my cash and knocked over the flour, and Dominique caught him in the act."

I pulled out my cell and called 911 for the second time that morning.

"Let's wait for the police outside," I said to Jenny and the others.

Jenny looked over at me with concern, then down at Dominique.

On instinct, my gaze fell to her hands to check for blood. Because *of course* she was the murderer. *Right?*

I wanted to ask how she could possibly miss the sounds of Dominique being stabbed, but I would leave that for Detective Trumble, the homicide detective from Whitney's murder.

Jenny whimpered from behind as we trailed behind Bethany and Angelina. On the way out, I reminded everyone not to touch anything. Out on the patio, the four of us met up with Tracy and Sweet Pea at a table. Sweet Pea pranced up to each of us with a quick lick.

"Do you want some ice water?" I asked Jenny. "I can run over to Confections."

"No," she said, shaken. Tears poured down her face.

Angelina reached into a pocket of her generously layered skirt and handed Jenny a tissue from a small packet.

Tracy helped settle Jenny into a patio chair, and Angelina laid one lace-gloved hand on her shoulder, swooping her long skirt aside and sitting next to her. Bethany paced up and down the sidewalk of Worth Avenue, her heels clacking on the concrete. *Clack, clack, clack.*

"Would you please stop?" I asked her, cranky from the anxiety pressing in on me.

Bethany, in her own world, ignored me.

Angelina, Tracy, and I exchanged glances and eyed Jenny, whose sobs had changed into hiccups.

"Why was Dominique here? I thought she was going home because her stomach hurt."

Jenny looked up at me with red-rimmed eyes and shook her head, breaking into sobs again. "I don't know."

Angelina laid a hand gently on the young woman's shoulder. "Maybe we should let her be for now," she said to me with her wind-chimes-blowing-in-the-breeze voice.

I sighed, impatient as ever to get to the bottom of it. I crossed one leg over the other and swung it up and down, leaning over to rub Sweet Pea's neck in time to my swinging leg.

Ten minutes later, the ambulance wheeled up, followed closely by Detective Trumble and his team. As lead homicide detective and possible paramour of my Aunt Mary, we had a bit of a past.

He greeted me with a gruff, "Samantha."

I nodded back and watched in awe as he took charge of the situation, barking orders to his team. The EMTs rushed inside. A couple of officers immediately pulled out yellow crime scene tape. My circle of friends and I skedaddled off of the pastry shop's patio as they began hanging the tape around the entire area.

Trumble said, "Everybody stay put. Wait next door at Bebe or go over to Confections."

Jenny and the rest of us looked at each other. Sweet Pea leaned her head forward to lick Trumble. He shook his hand away, then patted the top of her head before marching over to one of his guys.

The six of us—Sweet Pea, Jenny, Bethany, Angelina, Tracy, and me—wandered over to Confections with backward glances at the scene behind us. Twenty-year-old Jenny with the slender figure and surfer-girl style seemed like the last person to be involved in a murder, so naturally, her name zipped to the top of my list of suspects.

I leaned against a palm tree in front of Confections and gripped the handle of Sweet Pea's leash. With no husband or even a boyfriend waiting for me at home to talk all this through later, I leaned over and spoke into her folded ear. "You don't want to go home tonight and chat, do you?" She lolled her tongue at me and I couldn't help but smile. Who needed a cheating boyfriend when I had *this* fuzzy face at home?

Trumble, looking the quintessential Floridian in his pastel pink shirt, marched over to us under the canopy of Confections and called Jenny over to his squad car. Bethany, Angelina, and I smiled at her in a vote of confidence. Tracy, God love her, gave her a thumbs-up.

After Trumble took Jenny away, the rest of us got a grip by talking it out.

Bethany sat on the bench in front of Confections. "What the h—"

"I know," I said. "We're living in strange times."

Tracy said, "You're telling me."

Grateful I added patio tables to the front of Confections, not unlike Patisserie's, I plopped down next to Tracy. Sweet Pea circled and laid in a ball at our feet. Two shops over, a police officer spread his arms in front of the yellow tape, shooing away a couple of looky-loos.

"What do you think?" Bethany asked.

"It's surreal," Angelina offered from the other side of the table.

"Jenny said she didn't know what happened because she was busy in her back room," I explained.

"That could be," Tracy said, gesturing to the inside of Confections' display window. "I didn't know anyone had made a mess of the café until Samantha and I opened the front door this morning."

"What?" Bethany asked.

"Someone broke into Confections," I said. More like turned the doorknob but still ...

"Was anything missing?"

"Not that I know of."

The four of us stared at Trumble questioning Jenny in his squad car. No one said a word.

A car squealed up to the curb in front of Patisserie. I recognized some of the faces as the forensics team from Whitney's murder. They scattered out of the car in a flash and disappeared inside the pastry shop.

"It couldn't have been Jenny, right?" Angelina said. "I mean, if she wanted to kill Dominique, wouldn't she hide the body?" A stream of tears coursed down her cheeks. "I can't believe what I'm saying. 'Hide the body,' like it isn't our friend lying in there." She rummaged through her pockets. "I'm out of tissues. Do you mind if I run inside for a napkin?" she asked me.

Trumble faced away from us but I knew he had eyes in the back of his head.

"You better not," I commented.

"I'm okay," Angelina said and dried her face off with her lacy gloves.

Bethany said, "You certainly enjoy your accessories."

Angelina's forehead crinkled for a moment.

"What was Dominique doing in Patisserie, do you think?" Tracy asked us.

I said, "God, maybe she really *was* the thief and Jenny caught her in the act of stealing and had a fit of rage—"

"And killed her?" Angelina asked quietly. "You're saying two people who we consider friends are thieves and killers." Her gentle nature didn't accuse, only seemed genuinely affronted.

Trumble and Jenny exited the squad car. Jenny wandered back as Trumble stuck a lollipop in his mouth and gestured at me to join him.

Sweet Pea and I leaned against his squad car to avoid my pup's toenails tearing Trumble's fine, leather seats. "Weren't you supposed to be retiring soon?"

"Tell me what you know," he grumbled, ignoring my question, as usual.

I told him all of the details of my morning. Coffee klatch minus our usual Tracy, Angelina and Bethany. Dominique picking up a pumpkin before joining Jenny and me on Patisserie's patio, then complaining of an upset stomach. Dominique leaving us to go home, taking the short-cut through Patisserie to her car in the back.

"Did anything unusual happen aside from the three women not showing for coffee clutch?"

"Klatch."

"That's what I said. Coffee Clutch."

"No. It's an 'ah' sound. Like when the doctor wants to get a look at your sore throat." I opened my mouth. "Ahhhh …"

Trumble tensed his jaw. "Nothing unusual, then."

I reached down and rubbed the top of Sweet Pea's head. "Tracy was trying to surprise me with a whipped cream recipe, and I don't know why Bethany and Angelina didn't come. It's not like everybody comes every single time."

"You and Tracy were in your bakery—"

"It's a dog bakery." *You'd think he would know that by now.*

Louder, he said, "You and Tracy were in your *dog* bakery and heard a scream. That right?"

I nodded and chewed the inside of my mouth as I remembered that awful sound.

"You and Tracy ran over to Patisserie's patio, met up with Bethany and Angelina, and found Dominique on the floor with Jenny standing over her, right?"

"I think Angelina came a few seconds later than us, but yeah. And it's not like Jenny was standing over Dominique with a knife in her hand and a maniacal grin on her face. She was standing over Dominique sobbing."

I didn't even try to ask Trumble his take on my story. Why bother?

The Good Detective asked me more details: Did I touch anything, what all did I see in the pastry shop, did Jenny leave out the front door as soon as we called 911, like that. I answered to the best of my ability and he dismissed me a few minutes later, then marched back over to Confections' patio and called on Tracy, who trailed behind him.

"How did it go?" Bethany asked as I sat between Angelina and Jenny at the table.

"Alright," I said and glanced at Jenny.

"Where's Rick during all of this?" Bethany asked. "And what's going on with you two, by the way?"

"Nothing, I guess." And that was the truth. "I'm not anxious to dive into a new relationship after Peter, anyway."

Angelina asked, "Who is Peter?"

"Don't you remember?" Bethany asked. "He's the loser who broke her heart back in Sun Haven."

Angelina leaned over to me. "You don't have to dive into a new relationship."

Bethany said, "No. You don't have to dive in. Maybe just a dog paddle."

Meanwhile, Jenny sat sullen and quiet.

"Are you alright?" I asked.

"The detective said to stay here where he can keep an eye on me until he was finished with everyone." Her tanned face turned pale.

I tried to lift her up in the event that she hadn't killed Dominique. "Hey, when Whitney was found on my floor, everyone thought it was me, so don't feel bad if people start snapping pictures of Patisserie and pointing and whispering behind your back."

Jenny looked at me, horrified. "What?"

Bethany pointedly said to me, "Very helpful."

"If I killed Dominique, would I leave a dead body in my pastry shop?"

"It's easier than carting it away," Bethany answered.

"Geez, Bethany," I said. "Cold much? Dominique was our friend."

"You could be trying to outsmart us," Angelina said quietly. Her face shaded pink.

The three of us—Jenny, Bethany and me—gaped at Angelina. This, from the woman always filled with light and love.

"Oh my goddess, I'm sorry, Jenny," Angelina said. "Of course it's not you."

Jenny rubbed her forehead with the heels of her hands. "Detective Trumble said if they don't take me to the station now, chances are good he'll be calling me in again sometime."

I nodded and watched Tracy and Trumble trek back over to us. "He told me the same thing when I was in your shoes."

Tracy dropped into a chair. Sweet Pea jumped up and licked her ankle in greeting. She massaged my furry girl's head, neck, and body while Trumble called on Bethany.

After a few minutes, Bethany returned and Angelina joined the detective. As each woman trudged back, Sweet Pea greeted them with a lick on their calves or ankles.

At last, Trumble finished with us. He marched past Bethany's art gallery and over to Patisserie, where the EMTs carried Dominique out on a stretcher. Jenny, Bethany, Tracy, and I babbled nonsensically. Angelina stared at the stretcher with her usual poise.

Trumble spoke to a couple of his team members, then strode back over. Sweet Pea jumped up and wagged her tail. He nodded at her but didn't pet her. He was in pure business mode now ... his pink shirt—striped today—stuck to his chest from the early morning Florida sun already shining overhead.

"You're all free to go but nobody leave town."

"What about me?" Jenny asked. "I live in West Palm."

West Palm, maybe ten palm trees away from Palm Beach.

"So do I," said Angelina.

Trumble told them, "Don't leave West Palm either. You gave me your IDs, so I can track you down if you get any bright ideas." He unwrapped another Tootsie Pop and marched back to finish with his team at Patisserie.

Tracy asked, "Is he allowed to give them that order?"

Jenny ignored Tracy, lost in her own worries. "What am I supposed to do now?"

I needed to open Confections, and Bethany and Angelina were eyeing their shops, too. "I guess you should call the Goodwins and tell them what's going on since they're the ones who hired you to manage Patisserie."

Bethany said, "Whitney's parents are going to love this news."

"Yeah, only a month after their daughter was killed," I said.

"In your dog bakery," Tracy reminded me.

"Yes," I said. "I remember."

I put myself in Jenny's shoes, easy since I had been in them a month ago. "After they leave, which might be hours from now or even days—"

"Days?" Jenny asked.

"Depends on how complicated the crime scene is." I didn't know much, but I knew the basics. "First thing you'll probably want to do is clean the mess they leave. There's probably fingerprint powder all over everything. Then you'll want to check the locks."

"The locks are fine. The front and back doors were both unlocked when we were having coffee klatch."

Angelina stood up with the grace of a gazelle. "I'm sorry, all. I have to open my shop."

"Me too," said Bethany.

"Want us to walk you over to Patisserie?" I asked Jenny.

She nodded and Bethany, Tracy, Sweet Pea and I walked in the direction of Gallery Bebe to drop off Bethany and then Jenny.

"I can't believe Dominique caught the thief and he killed her," Bethany said.

I countered that with, "Or not."

Bethany said, "Right. Dominique could have been the thief and Jenny killed her."

Jenny's blue eyes opened wide.

"But you wouldn't have done that, right?" Tracy asked Jenny. She waited expectantly like Jenny would blurt out the truth.

Jenny stared blankly at Tracy. My assistant mumbled an apology, once again confused about what she had said this time. I grabbed her elbow lightly and guided her and Sweet Pea back over to Canine Confections before she could say anything else.

I turned the gold knob to Confections and opened the front door to the café as wide as it would go.

"Geez, really?" I said at what I found waiting for me in the café.

CHAPTER FOUR

O r rather *who* I found waiting for me in the café.

"Peter, what are you doing here?" I hadn't seen my old boyfriend for two months, ever since I left his sorry self back in Sun Haven.

My ex smiled at me from a café chair.

"This is Peter?" Tracy asked and began tidying up. "You didn't tell us he looks like Fabio."

Peter grinned even wider.

Surprised that Tracy knew Fabio, I said, "The only thing he has in common with Fabio is the suntan and long, blond hair. Anyone can have that with a trip to the drugstore and a day in the sun." Not everyone has the green eyes, sexy smile and sway of the hips like Peter, but no need to feed his already-overblown ego.

I unhooked Sweet Pea's leash. She took one whiff of Peter and padded back a few steps. Very unlike my girl, who normally licked everyone whether they liked it or not.

"I don't think she likes you," I said.

Peter had the same beachy vibe as Jenny, only Peter's hair grew wildly to his shoulders, while Jenny kept hers nice and neat, thanks to the Goodwin's request that she fit in with the Worth Avenue clientele.

He stood up and sauntered over. Between his slow smile and sexy swagger, my knees buckled.

I grabbed the top of a café chair, gathered myself up, and straightened my shoulders to look him squarely in the eye. "I asked what you're doing here."

"What do you think?" he asked softly.

The memory of finding him and Claire snuggling all cozy in the apartment he had begged me to move into was all the fuel I needed. "What makes you think you can just swagger back into my life?"

Not one to push—smooth talkers know that never works—he took a couple of steps back. An injured look crossed his face. "I just wanted to see you." Quieter, he said, "I missed you."

I wish I could say that I had learned my lesson, that I was too smart to fall for his charms again, but ... the ice in my veins defrosted a couple of degrees. And what was maddening ... he knew it. I could tell from the way he was biting his lip back from smiling.

I said, "You think you can just show up and I'll fall into your arms, don't you?"

His face grew serious again. I would *never* think that, it said.

Meanwhile, Tracy filled Sweet Pea's water bowl from behind the display case. "It's like that old disco song, 'I Will Survive.'" She laid my furry girl's bowl down and sloshed water on the floor as she sang, "So you felt like dropping in and just expect me to be free, well I'm saving all my loving for someone who's loving me, go on now go! Walk out—"

"Tracy!" I shouted above her loud singing. "Thanks! We got it!"

Peter raised his eyebrows at me in a question. *She for real?*

I checked the time. Our first customers would arrive at any minute.

Out on Worth Avenue, the ambulance and squad cars wheeled past the display window. A crowd from the direction of Patisserie came up to Confections' front door.

"I'm busy," I said to Peter. "You need to leave."

"Can I see you later?"

"No." I said this like I meant it. I wish I felt it, too.

Tracy traipsed over to the front door and held her hand at the lock. "You want me to let the customers in?"

Peter pleaded at me with his green eyes. "Come on, doll face."

I hated when he called me that. I found it degrading. *And yet.*

Damn.

Customers and pooches were pressing in at the window of the front door. I didn't have to ask why. They wanted the goods on what had happened at Patisserie and, since they probably got booted away from the pastry shop by the crime scene folks, they thought they could hear the gossip at my dog bakery. But I needed to get my business going in the right direction—away from ghost hunters and toward dog owners—before Aunt Mary's money flooded down the drain and she lost her estate.

Tracy asked, "Well? They're watching us …"

"Can we come in?" someone shouted through the glass door.

Peter's eyes fixed on mine. "Meet me for one cup of coffee?"

"I can get coffee here." *Well, espresso.*

"Hello!" someone shouted as though we didn't know they were three feet away.

Tracy said anxiously, "Samantha?"

Sweet Pea padded to the door and chuffed.

"One cup," Peter said.

"Geez," I said. "Okay. One cup." *In daylight. In public.*

Peter's face broke out in a smile. "You still have the same cell number?"

I nodded. "Now get out of here. I have to work."

He said, "I'm proud of you, Sam," and ambled out the door that Tracy had opened. The woman at the threshold didn't budge, forcing him to slide closely past her.

As I let our customers inside, Angelina across the street at Mystic Dreams opened the front door to her shop. Her flowing dress, lacy gloves, and hat seemed a little much for the Florida sun, but it suited the image of a New Age shop manager.

Ten or so customers filtered into Confections. Some even had a dog at their side. The rest ordered espressos and sat in the café.

"Can you believe another murder happened right here on Worth Avenue, of all places?" one said.

Another replied, "I know. As if this is *West* Palm Beach."

A man and a schnauzer strolled up to the display case. The man ordered a Peanut Butter Delight for Boopy, his schnauzer, and an espresso for himself.

Sweet Pea, having quickly learned to give our customers their space, waited for me to give her the okay to say hello to a customer and their Person.

"Here you go, Boopy," I said and handed the Delight to her owner. "I hope you like it." She wiggled her little tail and followed her Person to one of the only remaining seats in the café.

Sweet Pea pleaded at me with her big, brown eyes. "Half," I said and split a Delight in two. I smiled, in heaven that I had adopted her. Hard to believe that I had waited so long to adopt a dog.

"Peter is allergic to dogs, by the way," I said to Tracy, boxing up Pawfically Good Cupcakes for a woman and her two poodles. "By the time I felt I could afford to get one, I was dating Peter and by then, it was too late. Can you believe I let that happen? Chose him over a dog?"

Tracy bit her lip. "If you and he get back together, you wouldn't ..." she peered down at Sweet Pea with worry lines on her smooth forehead. She whispered and pointed at Sweet Pea. "Give Sweet Pea away?"

"Over my dead body."

Tracy blanched.

"Sorry," I said. "Poor choice of words."

"You said you're going to meet him," she said and sponged up the small sink behind the display case.

"Just coffee." I handed the woman the box of cupcakes and pulled over a bowl and a wooden spoon to mix up more Creamy Carrot Frosting.

"And that's it?" Tracy asked.

I thought about Peter and Claire in our apartment, and began stirring the frosting by hand with more force than necessary. The bowl of frosting flew off the counter and landed with a thud at Sweet Pea's paws.

I answered Tracy with a firm, "Absolutely. One ..." *Stir. Stir.* "Cup of coffee."

CHAPTER FIVE

Sweet Pea and I drove along Ocean Boulevard that Monday evening after our full day of coffee klatch, murder, and customers at Confections. Her black snout stuck out the passenger window and wiggled at the ocean air to our right. I stopped at a stoplight and waited for a man and woman in bathing suit coverups to cross the street to the beachside.

A few minutes later, we pulled up to my aunt's electronic gate. After I plugged in the code, it opened and I drove past the Big House on my left—Aunt Mary's mansion—then parked in front of the cottage my aunt lets us live in. Sweet Pea jumped out of the car, made her mark on the bougainvillea bush and sped inside.

After I fed her dinner, I left Sweet Pea in the air conditioning for my evening swim in the ocean. I had tried bringing her with me in the past, but she worried so much about me in the surf that I felt guilty. And she seemed fine with a little time on her own. That evening, I enjoyed my quick swim, returned to the cottage to Sweet Pea's wagging tail, and quickly changed into dry clothes.

We headed over to the Big House for cocktail half-hour with my aunt and when I didn't find her in the kitchen, I called out, "Aunt Mary?" *If she made her way up to the second floor without me ...*

I inhaled and exhaled deeply and looked at Sweet Pea, who stared back and wagged her tail as she waited for my next move.

I looked in the library, the patio, then my aunt's bedroom.

"I'm going to kill her," I said and pressed the elevator button.

If someone had told me I was going to regularly visit a mansion that had an elevator, I would have told them to find someone *else* to snooker. Aunt Mary was backing Canine Confections with what I found out *after* the fact—thank you very much, Aunt Mary—was her remaining savings. If it didn't succeed, my aunt was apt to lose her estate.

The elevator doors opened. Sweet Pea and I entered, and I pressed the number 2. We exited to find Aunt Mary stirring something in the glass pitcher.

"Don't even start," she called out before I said a word. "I need to get stronger and get my independence back."

"Your knee surgery—"

"Was two months ago. Even the surgeon said I should start walking as soon as I feel up to it."

Sweet Pea padded over and licked the bare knee below the hem of Aunt Mary's floral dress.

"Hello, sweet girl," my aunt said.

"How do I know if you feel up to it or if you're just impatient to get better?"

"Impatience runs in our family. I wouldn't talk if I were you."

Detective Trumble would agree. I sort of inserted myself into the case when Whitney's murder wasn't solved fast enough.

I ran over to help her with the cocktail. "Why don't you let me finish?"

"How many times have I told you to stop treating me like an invalid? I'm sixty-nine years old, not one hundred."

"But your knee—"

"Is getting better every day. Now sit down, and let me serve you for once."

I mumbled, "Somebody's feeling her oats," to Sweet Pea.

Aunt Mary poured something clear into tall glasses full of ice, and laughed. "There you go, talking like you're from the 1920s." She handed me a glass with a wedge of orange from the trees out back next to the tennis court. "Perrier today."

The cool glass in my hand felt comforting after the hot, hectic day.

Sweet Pea jumped up on the couch next to me, and my aunt and I settled into our daily roundup of the day's events. She told me that she drove herself to the grocery store to try picking up a few items for herself and brought them home to Chef Luca, her thrice-weekly chef.

"But he said he didn't need what I brought and told me that next time I should stay home and rest, that he had it handled."

I laughed. "Even Chef Luca is looking out for you!"

Aunt Mary's forehead furrowed into worry lines. "Maybe I insulted him, bringing food home for him to cook, as though I didn't trust him."

"Maybe you worry too much."

"Hello, Pot. Meet Kettle."

"Touché," I answered. "Speaking of worrying, I didn't want to bring this up but I guess I better before you find out from someone else."

She held her glass to her lips and waited.

"There was another murder on Worth Avenue this morning."

My aunt set her glass on the coaster on the rosewood table with a hard *clack*. "Not in Confections again?"

"No. At Patisserie."

"How awful!"

"Yup. That's one word for it."

"And in the Goodwins' pastry shop ... as if those two haven't had enough grief losing their daughter."

I drank greedily, bit into my orange, and tried to enjoy the cold juice down my throat to sweeten the harsh day. "They'll be okay. The girl they hired might not be."

"Jenny?"

"Yeah. She's the one who found Dominique lying on the floor."

"The jogger?"

I chuckled lightly. "Don't ever let anyone tell you there's anything wrong with *your* memory."

"Why would someone murder Dominique?"

Sweet Pea chuffed next to me.

"I don't know. There's a theory that she's the one who's been stealing from the shopkeepers and Jenny caught her and stabbed her."

My aunt's face grew pale.

I shot up from the couch and laid my hand on her forearm. "I'm sorry. I should have eased you into it."

She shook her head sadly and waved me away. I settled back next to Sweet Pea.

"There's no easing into this," Aunt Mary said.

I swirled the remainder of my orange slice around the Perrier in my glass. "I'd be surprised if that's what happened, though. I guess that's why I'm talking about it all nonchalant. Dominique lived here on Ocean Boulevard in a mansion. What did she need to steal for?"

Aunt Mary lifted her glass. "You know better than that, my dear niece. People don't always do things for obvious reasons." Smoothing the velvet couch with a slightly wrinkled hand, she said, "Maybe you should reach out to Jenny. She could probably use a friend."

Aunt Mary locked eyes with me until I nodded my head in an unspoken agreement that I would reach out to the girl.

"Watch your back, of course," she said firmly and sipped her cocktail.

We shared fewer laughs that cocktail half-hour. Mostly, we sipped and sat until our ride down the elevator to the cozy kitchen nook for dinner and puzzle time.

By the time Sweet Pea and I returned to the cottage an hour and a half later, I couldn't wait to wash the day off of me and snuggle with my furry girl. Soon as we arrived, she padded in a circle on top of our bed in that wolfy-circle thing dogs do to get comfy. Only she circled the top of a Neiman Marcus duvet cover instead of a bed of grass. I left her to it and showered, brushed my pearly whites, and set the air conditioning to freezing so I could cuddle up in my coziest flannel pajamas and fuzzy socks without burning up in the Florida humidity.

I turned the TV on to find the Cozi Channel, but paused at the panoramic views of beautiful Costa Rica on the Travel Channel. Andy Griffith would have to wait. The camera panned across a lot of the same lush trees and plants that grew in South Florida: tropical banana trees with yellow fruit that tastes sweet, manchineel "little green apple" trees that can kill people, and coconut trees with fruit in brown husks that require a hammer to open.

I pulled the comforter up to my chin and massaged Sweet Pea's fuzzy leg. The gentleman on TV chiseled open a coconut with forearms that glistened in the sun. This, of course, brought Peter's glistening skin to mind. I used to love watching him surf and especially loved when he would walk up to me from the ocean carrying his surfboard and smiling like he was ready for more fun—with me. I had forgotten to mention him to Aunt Mary. *Forgot, or didn't tell her on purpose?* I knew she wouldn't tell me what to do, but chances were excellent that she would subtly warn me to think twice before meeting him for that cup of coffee. *Come to think of it, how strange for him to show the day of Dominique's murder.* I threw that nugget out of my mind for the moment because I didn't want to hear it—even from myself—and left the Travel Channel in search of the Cozi station. On the way to finding it, I paused at a show called, *What Makes People Tick*. According to the episode, people are very complex. *No kidding.* It discussed everything from kleptomania to hoarding to obsessive-compulsive disorder, and presented them in a way to make it understandable why people sometimes do the things they do.

I turned off the TV and thought about how Jenny must be feeling. Unless she had killed Dominique, she was probably pretty scared. Remembering my aunt's prompting, I picked up my cell to at least text the girl. I kept my notifications off, so only then did I see the text from Jenny. She wanted to know if I would mind helping her chat her nerves away.

Along with Jenny's text, there were four from Peter: How's tomorrow for that coffee?

CHAPTER SIX

T he following morning, five of us had arrived at coffee klatch on Patisserie's patio. Me, Sweet Pea, Jenny, Tracy, and Bethany. No Angelina.

We reviewed the previous day's events. I apologized to Jenny for not receiving her text in time to return it before it was too late, and Bethany exclaimed, "Dominique probably never tried stealing from Bebe because of my extra bells and whistles package that I pay for with my security company. Can you imagine someone stealing the artwork in my gallery?"

"You're assuming Dominique was the thief," I said.

Tracy set her latte on the patio table. "You know, we're all calling this person a thief, but so far, no one has had much stolen. Only a little thing here and there, right?"

Bethany said, "Stolen is stolen. I don't care if it's a piece of art or a paper clip."

Jenny's eyes grew round, not yet accustomed to Bethany.

"Mind if I ask what's going on with Dominique?" I asked Jenny. "Have you heard anything?"

"Well, she's probably still dead," Tracy said.

Jenny looked at her, startled. She wasn't accustomed to *Tracy* yet, either.

Bethany, unfazed by Tracy said, "Trumble is probably working the case fast as he can. Which means *you* don't need to be involved this time." She gave me a pointed stare.

"Something you'd like to say, Bethany?" I asked.

"Yes, as a matter of fact. Trumble was doing a fine job of finding Whitney's killer. Why did you have to horn in on the case just because you were too impatient to wait until he finished wrapping it up?"

"Horn in? Isn't that type of talk a little pedestrian for you, Bethany? And I didn't exactly *ask* the murderer to come into my back room at Confections and try to hurt me."

"But you did egg her on at the get-together at Confections," Tracy said.

I shook my head at the two of them. "To bring things to a head! So that Whitney's killer could be brought to justice and my dog bakery could get up and running! My aunt's money is invested in this."

"Again with that?" asked Bethany. "I'm sure your aunt's estate is fine. You worry too much."

Tracy said softly, "I sort of get what Bethany means. You've been going on and on about your aunt's money that she invested in Canine Confections and what could happen if it doesn't succeed."

I felt, not a burn, but a low simmer. "I'm sorry if my consistent concerns are boring to you people."

"Samantha ..." Tracy said.

More on edge than I thought, I scanned the circle of faces and apologized.

Tracy said, "It's okay. You're just a worry-wart. And you're a little impatient."

I reached down and petted the furry girl at my feet. I didn't want to expand on the details of my aunt's money. It was her personal business. "It all ended okay."

"Except for the part where Whitney was murdered," Bethany said sarcastically. "Which by the way, I can't believe you brought a cannoli to her murderer in jail."

"Cannolo," I corrected. "One is called a cannolo."

"Is that true?" Jenny, the pastry shop manager asked.

"Yes," I said, suddenly wondering about her credentials, other than working at a bakery in Boca Raton and parents who know Whitney's mom and dad. "And for the record, I brought her more than one." *One pastry is a tease.* I sipped the frothy cream on my Starbucks cappuccino. "I love cinnamon."

Bethany said, "I miss the crisp fall air."

I would have asked her how she could miss something she never had here in Florida, except Bethany came from money. *Lots* of money. This allowed her to travel to places with cool air and colorful leaves whenever the mood struck.

The art gallery owner gazed across Worth Avenue and three shops down to Mystic Dreams. "Those two people are at Angelina's again."

Angelina was talking to a young woman and man. Both of them were lithe like her, but they were dressed in blue tee shirts and jeans, as opposed to Angelina's orange skirt and scarf.

"Customers?" Jenny asked.

"She doesn't open until ten," I answered.

Tracy said, "They don't look like customers. They look like they're giving her a hard time."

Bethany remarked, "For someone so enlightened, she doesn't seem all that confident. Have you seen how she reacts when I ask her about her crystals and cleansing and all that hooey?"

"Maybe you should stop calling it 'hooey,'" I said and smiled sweetly.

"Where's the fun in that?"

Back to the topic of Dominique, I asked Jenny, "Have you heard any news on Dominique's death yet? When she was killed? Who might have done it?" *Aside from you?* I neglected to add.

She shook her head. "Trumble is pretty tight-lipped."

Jenny and Bethany waved in the direction of Mystic Dreams. I turned in my seat as Angelina glided over in her cotton skirt and gypsy blouse.

"No hat and gloves today?" Bethany asked.

Angelina's face blushed. "One of these days, Bethany, I'm going to have a comeback line for you."

Bethany said, "You won't mind if I don't hold my breath." But she scooted over and pulled out a chair. The gallery owner was all bluff with no bite and Angelina was beginning to sense it.

Jenny pressed a hand to her forehead, trudged over to Patisserie's front door, and disappeared into her shop.

Angelina said, "Is anybody else worried about her headaches?"

"Actually, we're a little worried about you," I said. "Who are those two people that were just in front of your store?"

Angelina's face turned scarlet.

"You don't have to be embarrassed. Everybody has heated exchanges sometimes."

Bethany said to her, "Even you, Miss 'The World is a Beautiful Place.'"

"Bethany, leave her alone." I stood up to her like I did when she used to give Tracy a hard time.

An awkward silence filled the air as I tried to think of a new subject to let Angelina off the hook.

Jenny swung the front door of Patisserie open and plopped in her chair at the table. "Angelina, what's up with those people in front of Mystic Dreams?"

Tracy, Bethany, and I glared.

"What did I say?" Jenny asked, perplexed. "We were all wondering it."

Quickly, I changed the subject. "How's your head, Jenny?"

She gulped her water. "I just added orange juice instead of milk to my cup of tea. Don't ever get a concussion hitting your head on a surfboard."

Bethany said, "Maybe if you didn't try surfing when the weather forecasters told everybody to stay out of the rough waters …"

Jenny shrugged. "I like the challenge."

"You like the adrenaline of living on the edge," I said. "I don't know how you do it. You went rock climbing in Colorado—"

"And skydiving in Costa Rica …" Tracy offered.

Angelina added, "And parasailing in Mexico …"

Jenny laughed. "Shoot me for liking a little excitement in my life."

"A little?" I asked. "You told me you went white-water rafting without a life vest."

Bethany said, "Pretty stupid, if I can speak plainly."

"Since when are you afraid of speaking plainly?" I asked.

I missed my circle of friends in Sun Haven. Especially Claire, whom I had thought of as my best friend, and who wound up helping Peter cheat on me. That one really hurt.

"Maybe you created a new sensation … tea and orange juice!" Tracy offered.

Bethany smirked. "Not likely." To Jenny, "Head injuries can make you act and do things that are askew."

"Or cockeyed," I said.

Tracy asked, "I thought askew meant cockeyed?"

Bethany asked her, "Is that what happened to you?"

Tracy looked at her in puzzlement. "I never got hit on the he ..." she said, before she realized Bethany was giving her the business. Again.

It felt strange we should all be sitting there, in the spot where only yesterday morning, Dominique had stopped by after her jog, alive and mostly well. And now she was lying in the morgue, or wherever they kept her while finding out her time of death.

I stood up to leave, and Sweet Pea followed suit. "I have to check on my PawCakes."

Bethany scowled at something behind me. I didn't need to turn around to know what it was.

Or rather, *who*.

CHAPTER SEVEN

"You can't just keep showing up here," I said to Peter.

He shrugged and smiled. "You didn't return my texts."

"I'm not going to have coffee with you. I changed my mind."

"Come on. One cup of coffee isn't going to hurt anybody."

Sweet Pea chuffed at my feet.

"Tracy, want to help me with the PawCakes?"

She skedaddled up and out of her seat. "Sure! Here. I'll take Sweet Pea. Why don't you two ..."

I glared. Had the girl no sense of loyalty? This man had *hurt* me!

I handed Sweet Pea's leash to Tracy so that I could speak to Peter alone for a second while we headed over to Confections. I looked down past Rare Books and Stamps to Sophisticated Pet. *Where has Rick been, anyway?*

"Peter, I don't know why you've suddenly showed up here or what you want, but honestly, I can't be bothered."

He glanced behind me at the women I knew were watching our every move. "Can't we talk someplace private?"

"Absolutely not."

"What are you afraid of?"

"I see your ego hasn't lessened any since I found you with Claire."

His face fell. "About that. I'm sorry. I'm not with her anymore."

I can't say my stomach didn't kick up its heels in a happy dance. "That's a shame. What happened? She find out you're a cheating loser? Oh wait, so is she." I chewed the inside of my mouth. "She was my best friend. How could you two do that to me?"

He swept a hand through his blond hair, pulled back in a tight ponytail with an orange band. "I'm an idiot."

"We finally agree on something."

His gaze fell to Worth Avenue's sidewalk. "How are you doing? Are you okay?"

"I'm fine."

"What was going on here yesterday? The cop cars, ambulance?"

I glanced at Bethany heading to Gallery Bebe, shaking her head back and forth at me, and pursing her lips for me to stand strong. Angelina, crossing the street back to Mystic Dreams, glanced quickly away when I caught her staring. And Jenny cleared the patio table.

"No," I said to Peter. "You don't get to pretend everything is okay between us just like that."

"Have coffee with me."

Tracy exited Canine Confections and turned the sign to Open, then glanced at me.

"Fine," I said. *Anything to get him off my back.*

"Now."

"Do you think I can just drop everything for you?"

"I can't trust you to meet me later or return my texts. Come now."

"Yeah. That's not going to happen. I have a dog bakery to open."

"Lunch then. Where can we go around here?"

"I don't always take lunch breaks."

He scanned Worth Avenue and pointed at Taste of Tuscany a few shops down. "There. Are you able to meet me today at one o'clock?"

Inside the large, front window of Confections, Tracy stirred something in a bowl behind the display case. Probably Pawcake dough. Assuming she didn't add flaxseed or chia seeds or anything that didn't belong, it would be ready in plenty of time for our first customers in another half hour.

"I'll meet you there at one. Just stop showing up here." I walked away from him and entered Confections. Thank goodness, he strode down the avenue away from my shop.

"We're out of flour," Tracy called out as Sweet Pea ran over to say hello since she hadn't seen me in three minutes.

"How can that be?"

"Remember I tried to surprise you with the whipped cream yesterday? I may have used the last of it."

"Right. *Trace* ... we need it for the PawCakes."

"Sorry."

I opened the front door and waved it away. "I'll get a couple table-spoons from Jenny. Be right back. When you're done with that, order two more cases, would you please?" I thought about it. "On second thought, don't." Tracy had many good qualities. Using numbers was not among them.

I ran over to Patisserie and couldn't help staring at the spot on the floor where Dominique had been lying a day earlier.

Jenny stood at the back counter rolling out dough with a rolling pin. "What's up?"

"Do you have a couple of tablespoons of flour I can borrow?"

"Sure. It's right through there," she said and gestured with her chin to the swinging door between front and back. "Mind helping yourself? I sort of have my hands full."

"No problem." I led myself to the door. "Where is it?"

"Through there to the left."

I opened the door to her back room. Like mine, it had a walk-in refrigerator and closet. Unlike mine, stacks of pastry magazines sat in piles against the wall. I grabbed a bag of flour and returned to Jenny. "I see you're trying to teach yourself some new pastry tricks."

She studied the dough on the counter, sweat dripping down her face. "The magazines? Yeah. The Goodwins only hired me because they're friends with my parents. I don't want to make them sorry. I actually love this stuff!"

I looked at the ooey-gooey goodness on her counter and laughed. "Yeah. Me too." Plus, I had the added pleasure of having dogs around every day.

"I only need a little of this. I should have brought a baggie."

She dismissed that. "Just bring back what you don't use. So what happened with Peter?"

"Do we really all have to know each other's business in our little group?" I said, only half-kidding. "I know Bethany doesn't think I should give him the time of day. And she's probably right."

"She's just looking out for you."

"I told him I'd meet him for lunch."

Jenny stopped rolling the dough. "You did?"

"Not one of my proudest moments."

She shrugged. "If it makes you feel any better, I can see why. He's pretty easy on the eyes."

"I know. But more than that, I keep remembering how sweet he can be. He was really good to me when I was going through a rough time." He had been there when the mortgage crisis almost cost my parents their house, and I had to give them my savings for a dog bakery I wanted to open.

I opened the front door and held up the flour. "I'll bring you a fresh bag."

"It's weird though, isn't it?" Jenny asked, her face pinched with two frown lines between her eyebrows.

"What's weird?"

"Peter showing up the day Dominique got killed."

CHAPTER EIGHT

I returned to Confections with the flour, then grabbed the powdered sugar, ready to whip up a delicious frosting for my customers. Normally, I liked using the tiniest bit of honey because sugar is no better for dogs than it is humans, but a small amount would be alright.

Soon as I opened the door, Sweet Pea ran over to say hello to me again, and a brown-haired, stubble-faced, sophisticated guy smiled at me from in front of the display case.

"Hey, stranger," he said.

My stomach flipped, and not like with Peter. This time, it swirled and swooped, too. Not one to go weak in the knees for just any old guy, I was in unchartered territory. The last date I had in fact, was with the guy standing in front of me.

"Hello stranger to you too," I said.

Tracy beamed at me from behind the display case.

"Tracy, here's the flour. Want to finish that up in the back please? It'll make less of a mess when the customers start coming in."

She grinned, grabbed her bowl, beaters, and flour. "No problem!"

"And remember, flour doesn't go in the whipped cream," I reminded her before turning my attention to Rick. "So," I said. *I see the stubble on your cheeks is as sexy as ever.*

"So," he said and smiled. "I hear we had some excitement again."

"Dominique. Yeah. We missed you at coffee klatch the past couple of days."

"I don't usually go to coffee klatch with you."

"You know what I mean. I haven't seen much of you. I thought you might have come around to check on all the hub bub."

I motioned for him to join me at a café table and gazed out at Worth Avenue to gather myself. Bethany and Jenny were chatting. Strange, since they both had shops to open and Jenny seemed busy with her dough a moment ago. Angelina's front door stood ajar. She draped a scarf over a Buddha statue in her display window.

Rick sat down. Sweet Pea nudged her muzzle to him. He returned her affection by petting her fluffy head.

"Do you want something? Water, espresso?"

"When are you going to start serving something more than espresso for your human customers?"

"I'm not sure that I'm ready to expand my menu yet."

"Okay, change of subject. Have the police figured out what happened to Dominique?"

I didn't want to tell tales but so far, it looked like Jenny had killed her while catching her stealing from her petty cash. My ability to go over to Jenny and ask for flour, as if all was right with the world, made me wonder about myself.

"There's a possibility that Dominique is the one who was stealing…"

I jumped when Confections' front door flew open. Angelina raced inside. Sweet Pea ran over to her, sniffed, and licked my new friend's ankles.

"Angelina! How …? What happened?"

Her hair hung in an unruly swirl around her face and her skirt twisted around her waist like a snake with its prey. "Did you see …" She stopped when she saw Rick. "Oh. I'm sorry. I didn't mean to interrupt—"

"It's no problem," I said. "What's wrong?"

She glanced at Rick and said quietly to me, "Did you see anyone run in front of your sidewalk just now?"

"I don't think so. Then again, I've been pretty busy …" *Mesmerized by the perfect man sitting in my dog bakery café.*

Rick asked, "What happened?"

"I was finishing up with my Buddha and setting up the display of crystals. I ran to my desk for the magnifying glass and when I returned to the front, my precious crystal collection was gone. My boss is going to kill me. Someone came in and stole it!"

I gasped. "Are you sure?"

Angelina started weeping quietly. "Yes."

If the thief was still out there, Dominique was innocent. Jenny would be glad at least that it let her off the hook a little for having motive to kill her. But the rest of us? I turned to Rick and Angelina. "That means we have not only a thief, but a murderer running loose and no idea who it is."

CHAPTER NINE

A ngelina couldn't seem to catch her breath from the tears.

Rick said, "I have to open my shop, but anything I can do here?"

"No," I said. "You go on ahead." He made me nervous anyway, all chiseled chin stubble and perfect manners.

I handed Angelina some water. "Here. Drink this slowly."

She gulped it down. "I'm so sorry. This isn't like me. I normally have a better handle on things."

"Welcome to the club," I said. "The Worth Avenue club, where you always have to watch your back."

She raised her eyebrows and stared at me.

"I hear it's not always like this," I offered. "I've only been here for a month, but so far, this is the second murder." I sat quietly for a moment and digested this. Softly, I said, "Are you absolutely sure the crystals were stolen? You didn't misplace them?"

"I'm sure. They were there, and then they weren't."

"Could it have been those two people that we see from time to time outside of Mystic? Maybe we should look into them."

Angelina straightened her shoulders, wiped her tears and stood. "No. I am so sorry, Samantha. I'm fine." Back to her usual all-is-well self. "I've taken enough of your time. What's going on with you and Rick?" she asked, deftly changing the subject. She seemed much better than a minute ago, like flicking a switch.

"Your guess is as good as mine. You're okay now to go back and open Mystic?"

Angelina waved my concern away. "Oh yeah. I took acting in high school. I played the heck out of Scarlett O'Hara in *Gone with The Wind.*"

"A high school stage play of *Gone with the Wind*? You must have had one ambitious drama teacher."

She smiled and started to respond, but Tracy burst out of the back room.

"Where did he go?" she cried.

"Who?" I asked.

"Rick."

"He left."

"Oh," she said, disappointed.

"I have to open," Angelina said. "See you two later."

"What was that all about?" Tracy asked when Angelina left.

"She thinks someone stole something just now from her store."

"That means that Dominique wasn't the thief! Thank goodness!"

I headed to the counter to whip some more cream and get in my happy zone. "It means there is a thief and murderer out there."

Tracy joined me at the counter and pulled over the electric mixer. "Wasn't there always a murderer out there?" she asked innocently, unfazed.

"At least before, we thought it was Jenny."

Tracy looked at me, horrified. "We did?"

"Yes."

"Then how could you go over there and borrow flour like everything was—"

"Excellent question."

I'll give you that answer as soon as I figure it out myself.

CHAPTER TEN

My lunch break with Peter flew by. A cinnamon-scented candle sat with a low flame between us. The candlelight cast an attractive glow on the guy who didn't need help looking attractive. Peter kept bringing up our best moments together, and I ate it like candy. Inviting me to a fine-dining restaurant and remembering that Italian is my favorite were two little checks in the plus column for my ex.

At the end of the hour, when the waiter came with our check, Peter reached into his pocket and pulled out a hairband with blond tendrils trailing.

"My wallet is missing. Think you can cover my lunch?"

"You're not serious."

"Afraid so." He reached into his other pockets. "Somebody must have stolen it."

The thought crossed my mind that the thief could have stolen it, but it wasn't likely. "Did he reach into your pocket and pull your wallet out without you noticing it?"

"I must have dropped it."

I paid the bill, adding an extra tip for the waiter, then got up to leave. *Enough was enough of this guy.*

"Good-bye, Peter."

He followed me out the door to Worth Avenue.

"I'm not going to chase you down the street," he said.

"Good to know. And don't come near me again."

A passerby glanced at us and, with perfect Palm Beach manners, averted her gaze to a shop window.

I spent the rest of the afternoon at Confections mixing sweet treats and laughing at the ghost and mummy bandanas on the dogs whose owners must have been eager to begin the Halloween season. The dogs pranced into the café like they were the most loved pet in all the world. It lifted my spirits considerably.

At the end of the day, I drove with Sweet Pea along Ocean Boulevard and pulled up to Aunt Mary's gate, eager for a cozy evening at home.

I drove past the mansion and raised my eyebrows at Detective Trumble's Buick. I parked in front of the cottage, let Sweet Pea jump out of the car off the leash since we were safely tucked in to the estate, and traipsed over to check on Aunt Mary. I would have knocked, but chances were excellent that she and Trumble were nowhere near the front door. Instead, I opened the door wide into the foyer and scanned the hallways for signs of movement or sound. When none came, I called out, "Aunt Mary? Are you okay?"

"In here!" she trilled from the kitchen.

Sweet Pea and I strolled into the massive kitchen to find my aunt and Trumble standing over the stove with a wooden spoon and a spatula. Both were sweating from the steam pouring out the top of a pot.

"What are you guys up to?"

"Making lemon merengue pie from scratch."

Aunt Mary had told me Trumble sometimes came over for pie, but I had never witnessed it. I felt slightly ... odd.

"How cozy of you," I said.

Trumble's slack jaw and pink shirtsleeves rolled up to his elbows made him look—dare I say—relaxed.

"Detective, you look ..."

He twisted his head to glare at me.

"I was just going to say, you look very comfortable at the stove. Maybe a career as a chef is in your future after you retire from police-detecting."

"Oh, he's not retiring anytime soon!" Aunt Mary said.

Trumble glanced at her and flashed his eyes at me.

Aunt Mary stopped, as though she had said something she shouldn't.

"I'll leave you two, then," I said. "I just wanted to make sure everything was okay. And I guess cocktail half-hour is off?"

Trumble asked, "Cocktail *half*-hour?"

"By the time I get home from Confections in the evenings, Aunt Mary and I are usually too famished to sit for a full cocktail *hour*," I explained.

Aunt Mary asked me, "Meet me back here for puzzles later?"

"Sounds good."

I led Sweet Pea out of the kitchen, through the massive foyer, and out the front door onto the grounds of the estate. "Well," I said to her. "That's a fine howdy-do." She looked up at me with her big browns and lolled her tongue.

Once in the cottage, I fed the girl, changed into my bathing suit, and kissed her nose before jogging the quarter mile to the beach. The waves caressed my body, and I could literally *feel* the nerves release from my neck and shoulders, like releasing a helium balloon. By the time the sun set, my body felt like Jell-O. In the dusk, I waded out of the ocean. Up on the sand, I spotted somebody fully clothed and unmoving. Goosebumps crept from my feet up through my legs, belly, and the back of my neck. By the time my feet sank into the wet sand, the figure turned around and trudged up the dry sand. I jogged as quickly as I could to catch up, but by the time I reached Ocean Boulevard, all I could make out was a person rounding the corner, much too far away to decipher whether it was a man or woman.

I raced back to Whitehall, peering over my shoulder every thirty seconds or so. The goosebumps didn't abate. I pressed the electronic gate and clicked it shut, hoping Trumble hadn't yet left. Walking quickly on the long driveway toward the mansion, I sighed at the empty spot where his car had been only half an hour earlier.

After a quick dinner in the cottage, Sweet Pea and I returned to the Big House for puzzles and our daily catch-up with Aunt Mary, especially important since we had missed our cocktail time. I found my aunt sipping a cup of tea and snapping a puzzle piece into place, the scent of lemons in the air.

"Oh, yes!" she said and clapped her hands together.

"Where's Trumble?"

"He had to leave. Would you like some pie? It hasn't completely set yet but you can spoon out some if you want."

The merengue on the pie on top of the stove stood in high peaks.

"I'll wait. It's too pretty to mess up before it's ready." I didn't mention the beach because I didn't want to spoil her mood, especially since the beach-lurker was probably no one I needed to worry about. I pulled out my crossword puzzle book and made myself a cup of tea. After a few minutes of silent concentration on our puzzles, I asked, "Did Trumble tell you anything about Dominique's death?"

She snapped another piece in place. "What makes you think he tells me anything?"

"Aren't you two ... you know? An item?"

"An item?" Aunt Mary chuckled, then furrowed her brow at the puzzle on the table that, so far, looked like it might be a picture of a large bee landing on a pink flower. "It's a shame that Dominique suffered so much before being killed."

"I thought you said he didn't tell you anything."

"I didn't say that. I asked what makes you think he would." She chuckled and sipped her tea. "He didn't say much. I could tell from the way he answered, when I asked if she suffered. Normally when I ask questions, he politely tells me it's police business. This time …"

"What?"

My aunt blinked and hesitated a moment. Quietly, she said, "He said she had blisters on her mouth and hands, and he wouldn't know the cause until after the autopsy. Then he clamped his mouth shut, shook his head, and mumbled something about losing his edge, that maybe he should retire."

"I noticed the blisters too. I thought they were from tennis."

"Around her mouth?"

"Sun poisoning. We're in Florida."

We both sighed and resumed our puzzles and tea. Afterward, Aunt Mary slid two pieces of pie on a plate for me to bring to the cottage, and Sweet Pea and I left. On our way from the mansion to our cozy home, a sense of dread returned.

I jumped at a creak of tree branches overhead. "Did you hear that?" I asked Sweet Pea.

She panted her reply and sniffed the stone walls that separated Whitehall from the estate next door. Except for the sliver of moonlight, darkness enveloped us. And even though we were probably safe on the estate, a spray of goosebumps prickled my neck.

All of a sudden, Sweet Pea took off.

"Sweet Pea! What are you doing? Sweet Pea!"

I heard a scuffle of branches and she ran back, panting and wagging her tail.

"Where were you? You need to come when I call you!"

She looked up at me with eyes that shimmered from the moonlight and seemed to say, "I did. See? Here I am."

"Thank you, but next time listen sooner. You freaked me out."

I listened for unusual sounds. Nothing but the soft chirping of crickets and the occasional car on Ocean Avenue. In the gaps between crickets and cars, I heard the ocean waves. Thanks to Whitney's murder, Trumble's cell phone number was in my list of contacts. I took my chances and called on my way into the cottage, then locked and bolted the front door behind us.

"Hey," I said. "Sorry to bug you."

"Mary okay?"

I smiled at his first concern.

"She's fine."

"You know I didn't give you my number so you could have the police on your own personal speed dial, right?"

"Sorry, yeah. It's probably my imagination, but I just thought you might want to know ... I was swimming at the beach, and I thought I saw someone."

"What happened?"

"Nothing happened."

"But you saw someone."

"Yeah."

"At the beach." His tone took on a frustrated edge.

"Yes. But it was the way he or she was standing. I think he had clothes on instead of a bathing suit, and he stood there until I came out of the water. Then he walked away."

Silence from Trumble at the other end of my cell. Then, "Think I should put out an alert?"

"Very funny."

"It was a man?"

"Huh?"

"You said *he* had clothes on and walked away. It was a man?"

"I don't know. I couldn't tell. I was out in the ocean." I peeked out the curtain into the darkness. "And also, Sweet Pea just chased someone on the estate."

"Someone?"

"Yeah."

"Man? Woman? Someone wearing clothes?"

"Alright, I know how this sounds but ..."

I shut all of the curtains in the kitchen and living room, and refreshed Sweet Pea's bowl of water.

"I think somebody's imagination is getting the best of her," Trumble said. "Can't say I blame you. But let us do our jobs, and we'll bring in Dominique's murderer quicker than you can say uncle."

"What does that mean? 'Say uncle?'"

He grumbled something and hung up.

Chances were good that Trumble was correct, and I only had the heebie-jeebies. But chances were also good that someone was, for some reason, keeping their eye on me and everyone else on our little strip of Worth Avenue. My next step was finding out exactly who that someone was.

CHAPTER ELEVEN

Wednesday morning, I arrived with Sweet Pea at Canine Confections with a brand-new attitude and a small pumpkin for each café table.

I unhooked her leash and set to work placing one gourd per table, knowing that Tracy might move them. She might pile them in a pretty heap off to the side. Or maybe she would carve jack-o-lanterns and set a tiny candle in each one. It didn't matter. Whatever she came up with, it would be great. I could almost feel the stress of the past few days leave my body. Maybe Angelina was onto something with all of her positive attitude and flowing energy stuff.

Two days ago, Dominique was murdered. Yesterday, Rick showed up with no explanation of where he had been, not that he owed me one. Nor did he mention why he hadn't asked me out for a second date. And if he didn't want to go on a second date, neither did I. How's that for acting like a teenager in a twenty-seven-year-old body?

After I set the pumpkins on the tables, Sweet Pea and I joined the group at Patisserie for coffee klatch, where the four women chattered in a blur of cross-talk about who killed Dominique now that Jenny hadn't murdered her for thievery.

"So, you guys all thought I was the one who killed her?" Jenny asked.

Me, Tracy, Bethany, and Angelina looked at each other, then at Jenny.

"Sorry," I said.

"Thanks."

Bethany offered, "If it makes you feel any better, Samantha, me, and Tracy all thought each other killed Whitney."

Tracy's glossy, orange nails glimmered in the early morning sun as she twirled her ponytail with her index finger. "And Samantha thought I was spying on her for *Pulse on Palm Beach*."

Jenny asked, "Palm Beach's version of *National Enquirer*?"

Tracy nodded and lightly shoved her shoulder against mine in a playful gesture. "And now we're the best of friends."

"Ummm ... yeah," I said and smiled at Tracy. Actually, she probably *was* the best new friend I had made in Palm Beach since moving here a couple of months ago. *She probably wouldn't cheat on me with Peter, at any rate ...*

"Earth to Samantha?" Bethany said and clicked her fingers in front of my eyes.

I snapped to attention.

"We were just saying that you and Jenny have a lot in common," Bethany said. "You both own a bakery—"

"Mine is for dogs—" I said.

"And I don't own Patisserie, I only manage it," Jenny said. "Plus, it's a pastry shop, not a bakery."

Exasperated that we had ruined her point, Bethany continued. "Whatever. Bakery, pastry shop."

Jenny leaned over and scruffed Sweet Pea's ears. "But Samantha and I do have a lot in common. For one thing, I love dogs."

"I love dogs, too," Tracy proclaimed.

"It's not a competition, guys," I said and laughed.

Bethany tapped her elbow to Jenny's. "Maybe it is."

Jenny returned the bump with one of her own. "You hit me, I hit you," Jenny said and grinned.

The art gallery owner threw her a dirty look.

"Bethany can dish it out," I said, "but she can't take it."

Angelina finally joined the conversation and said softly, "Leave Bethany alone."

"This, from the woman who Bethany regularly makes fun of for cleansing Mystic Dreams with sage?" I asked.

Tracy set her iced coffee on the table with a *clank*. "I heard they think the blisters on Dominique were related to her death."

We all turned to Little Miss Ponytail.

I knew from Aunt Mary that Trumble had mentioned that, but how did Tracy know? "Let me guess. Someone at *Pulse* told you?"

She nodded. "I have a few little birds tweeting in my ear, yeah."

"More like tweeted on Twitter," Bethany said.

Tracy's eyes took on a pained expression but this time, it only lasted a moment before she returned to her normal, happy self. *Good for you, Trace.*

Tracy expanded. "They think somebody did something that would make her mouth and fingers blister. Only they have no idea what."

"But she was stabbed," I said. "What would one thing have to do with another?"

"Can we please stop all of this morbid talk about death?" Angelina asked. Her face took on a pale tone, not unlike Jenny's. The poor women didn't know what they were getting themselves into when taking jobs on our strip of Worth Avenue.

"I second that," said Jenny. "I have some fresh croissants inside. Come in and help yourselves before you leave."

My eyes followed a woman who had strolled past Rare Books and Stamps and stopped in front of Sophisticated Pet. She disappeared inside the pet boutique.

"Who's for a buttery, chocolate croissant?" Jenny asked and popped up out of her patio chair.

"I could use something sweet," I said.

We all went inside Patisserie except Angelina, who didn't want to be tempted by the sugary scent in the pastry shop. She said she had recently finished a juice cleanse and didn't want to "dirty" herself. Her words.

Jenny tried to make nice with Tracy, who was acting like a child, thinking she was in competition for my friendship. Bowls of bananas, apples, lemons, limes and two different types of avocados sat on top of the display case.

"Martha never had those," Bethany said and pointed to a multi-colored fruit tart in the glass case.

"Look at her," I said and motioned to Jenny's beach body. "Does she not look like all she eats are fruits and salads?" I eyed the gallery owner's svelte figure. "Look who I'm talking to. Is everyone around here a size two?"

While Bethany and I gazed longingly at the display case, Tracy salivated at the croissants Jenny packaged up for her. Sweet Pea salivated along with her.

"No chocolate for her," I said to Tracy.

"I wouldn't give chocolate to a dog," Tracy said.

"I know. Don't mind me, you know I'm a worry-wart." I also knew Tracy forgot stuff from time to time.

Patisserie's landline rang. Jenny picked it up on the second ring. "I can't talk now, Mother. I have customers." Jenny's face drew into a frown. "Can I call you back?"

Another moment, and Jenny hung up.

"Mommy, huh?" Bethany said.

"She heard about the murder and wants me to move back home." She pressed her index fingers to her temples.

"How old are you again?" Bethany said.

I squeezed Bethany's arm, reminding her to be quiet for once in her life.

We left Patisserie soon after the phone call, and it made me thankful for my own mother and father, an hour and a half southwest of Palm Beach and only too happy to see me building my own business ... though it was thanks to Aunt Mary's money.

On my way back to Confections, I peeked down at Sophisticated Pet to see if the woman who had entered Rick's store emerged, then looked over at Mystic's open door. "Trace," I said. "Take my croissant, please. I'll be there in a minute. And don't eat it."

I strolled across Worth Avenue with Sweet Pea to Mystic Dreams. Upon entering the store, I called out, "Angelina? Is it okay if Sweet Pea comes in?"

She sailed out from the back, all flowing skirts and dangling earrings. She wore velvet gloves. Scattered across a front table were stones and gems. Incense sticks stood tall as soldiers. Angelina's hands shook slightly, but she lowered her face to a plant and breathed in, then pursed her lips and exhaled slowly.

"What are you doing there?" I asked.

"Rosemary. Here, smell." She handed me the potted plant.

I breathed in and instantly felt uplifted. "Delicious. Makes me want to cook roasted potatoes."

I lowered the herb to Sweet Pea, who sniffed and sneezed.

"Too strong for you?" I said to the girl and rubbed her wiggly body.

Plenty of other items lay scattered on shelves and tables. Candles flickered, their shadows dancing on the walls. New Age music with a harp and cello played softly in the background.

"What's this doohickey?" I asked and picked up a strange-looking dry cluster.

"That's the sage," she said. "It's the one I told you guys about. You smudge your house with it and it cleanses the energy."

"How does that work exactly?"

"Ask the quantum physicists. Everything is energy."

I took her word for it.

"Angelina, the reason I came over was to see if you are okay. I know it's been a rough few days."

"More than a few days," she said. "The area has been having break-ins for a couple of weeks now."

"The police call it criminal mischief when nothing is stolen."

"Well, my crystals were stolen."

"And so was Jenny's petty cash."

She lifted her arm to run her fingers through a windchime. Her bell sleeve flowed downward in a graceful arc.

I asked, "Have you always dressed …" I stopped when she directed her gaze at me like I was accusing her of something. "I just mean … it's very pretty. I was never very good with fashion. Or anything visual. Tracy is the one who decorated my dog bakery."

Angelina's shoulders drew down from her head and she breathed in deeply. "She's done great work. Is she the one who hung all the big pictures on your walls of dogs eating ice cream cones and cupcakes?"

I chuckled and petted Sweet Pea's head. Hearing our comfortable tone, she laid down with her chin on the floor.

"No, the photos were my idea. And my aunt helped pick out the floral material for the bench cushions and the Michael Aram napkin holders on the café tables."

Angelina tilted her head. "Then what is it Tracy *did,* exactly?"

"Oh!" I laughed. "She did a lot. She is the one who came up with the layout of the snacks in the display case and the lighting, angling it so it's not right in the customers' faces ..."

"Customers meaning dogs."

"Yes. And people. I mean, we do have espresso ... how about you?"

"Me? We don't serve food."

"Yeah. No. I mean, are you happy here?"

"At Mystic Dreams? Yes, I've never been so happy. My boss hardly ever comes around and when he does, he seems pleased with the job I'm doing."

"That's great. I just wanted to check on you ... I know when I arrived a month ago and so much happened, I felt pretty lonely and scared. If you ever feel that way, you can always call me, okay?"

She swept her fingers through a bowl of dried potpourri. "Thank you, Samantha."

We said good-bye, and Sweet Pea and I padded across the street.

I entered Confections' café and heaved a sigh at Tracy, sweating and searching the bench cushions like the Mad Hatter.

CHAPTER TWELVE

"What are you looking for?" I asked and unclipped Sweet Pea's leash.

"A napkin holder is missing."

I felt the color drain from my face. "Those things are over a hundred dollars each."

I joined Tracy lifting cushions as if the napkin holder would have somehow miraculously lifted the cushion and slid itself underneath.

"When did you notice it was missing?"

"About ten minutes ago," she said and ducked her head down to check under a bench cushion. "I was in the back getting things ready for today's opening after coffee klatch, and I came up to take a look at your pumpkins. Do you want them just sitting there in the middle of the tables like that?"

"We can talk about the pumpkins later." I lifted my cell out of my pocket.

"Who are you calling?"

"Trumble."

"For a missing napkin holder?"

"I just want to find out how long we have to wait before they put someone on alert here."

Tracy plopped onto a bench cushion and sighed. "You think they'll run over here for a missing napkin holder?"

I bit my lip. The police had more important things to worry about, like a murder to solve.

She asked, "And didn't they say it was criminal mischief and they can't put police protection on us for that?"

When Tracy is the voice of reason, I'm in trouble.

I laid my phone down on the counter next to the mixer and set to work on the morning PupTarts while I thought of my next move. Tracy popped up off the bench and joined me. We got a nice little rhythm going, Tracy mixing, me pouring batter into the molds.

"I never did ask," she said. "How did lunch with Peter go yesterday?"

"He forgot his wallet."

"He must have felt awful," Tracy said.

I turned to her, wondering how she managed to make it to her mid-twenties without someone selling her swampland under the guise of a tropical island.

"Tracy, he did it on purpose."

"No. How do you know that?"

"Because I know Peter. Not that he's ever done exactly that." I leveled the batter in the mold. "Actually, he didn't say he forgot it. He said it was stolen."

She gasped and rested the mixer on top of the bowl of remaining dough. "Well, there you go! And it's another theft!"

"How do you suppose someone stole it from his pants pocket while he was wearing them? Come on, Tracy, even you can't be that naive."

Her eyes welled up.

"Oh, God. Stop. Don't you dare cry because I'm being a witch."

"I guess I should toughen up." She sniffled and straightened her shoulders. "It could have fallen out of his pocket. Haven't you ever lost a cell phone or something?"

I nodded. "In the washing machine when I forgot to take it out of my pocket first." I paused. "Okay. Maybe I'll give him another chance."

"What about Rick?"

"What about him?" He seemed busy with someone, Miss *lady knocking at his front door before the shops were open this morning.*

"I've known him all through school. He seems to like you."

"Me and everyone else," I mumbled.

"What?"

The door flew open. Sweet Pea stood up and tentatively wagged her tail.

"Hello, Ladies," Peter said, ponytail and smile in place. He directed his gaze at me. The smile faltered as if his confidence wavered. Classic ladies' man move. Softly, he said, "How are you?"

I chewed the inside of my mouth, willing myself to resist him. "Tracy, would you please finish up here?"

I guided Peter to a corner table of the café and twirled the stem of a pumpkin back and forth so the pumpkin twirled too. "What do you want, Peter?"

"I took a chance you might want to see me."

"Considering the last time we saw each other I told you never to come near me again, that's pretty risky of you."

He chuckled that stupid soft noise that made my stomach turn to mush. "Risky? What … you're going to hurt me?" Peter's lips curved up into a small smile. Coyly, he said, "I trust you."

"Yeah, well I don't trust you. You've been giving me more attention than you did in the five years we spent together. It can't be as simple as you want the girl you lost, can it?"

"I want to take you to HMF tonight at The Breakers."

"I've been there." *With Rick.*

My cell rang. I pulled it out of my pocket and blinked at Bethany's name glaring up at me.

"Hold on," I said to Peter, who was trying to get Sweet Pea to lick him.

On the other end of the phone Bethany said, "You may as well let this play out. We all know you're going to go out with him a few times, see he's the same no-good louse, and dump him. May as well get it done so you can move on."

I opened the front door and turned to Gallery Bebe. Bethany leaned against her front window, talking on her cell phone. I couldn't make out the expression on her face from Confections, but she stood with one hand on her hip and one high-heel sandal crossed in front of the other.

"Don't you have anything better to do than worry about my love life?" I asked.

"Unfortunately, not at the moment."

I hung up with Bethany, went back inside, and asked Peter, "Want to tell me why you showed up the day you did?"

"I wanted to see you in person instead of just calling."

"I know. But why that day? The day Dominique was killed?"

"You expect me to answer that?"

"It can't be a coincidence."

"Sure it can." He got up from the table, moseyed over to the front door, grinned that half-grin that made my insides squirm and said, "Let me take you to dinner."

"No."

"A drink at least. And music. At HMF tonight. Alright?"

I sighed. "Fine. I'll meet you at The Breakers."

"Can't wait."

He slipped out the door to the front sidewalk.

"Arrogant jerk," I said aloud.

Tracy said from behind the display case, "Yeah, but he's one cute arrogant jerk."

"Why do you think I have such a hard time letting him go?" I muttered.

"Bad boys," Tracy said and shook her head. "What is it about them that makes them so hard to resist?"

Sweet Pea walked over to her bed behind the display case, curled in a ball for a snooze, and chuffed.

"I couldn't agree more," I replied to her.

I fiddled with a pumpkin and thought about how difficult it would be to carve a face unless someone was very good with a paring knife. "Hey, Tracy? How did the napkin holder get stolen, anyway? I know we didn't leave the front door unlocked all night again, because I double-checked last night."

She brushed a loose strand of hair with the back of her hand and joined me in the café. "It must have been sometime this morning. You opened before going to coffee klatch and didn't lock up, right?"

I sighed. *Brilliant, Samantha.*

Tracy finished, "When I came back here after coffee, I didn't lock the front door when I was working in the back because I didn't think I needed to." She frowned.

"What now?" I asked.

"I ran to my car because I left my yogurt that I brought for lunch."

"So, someone could have come in either while you were in the back or when you ran to your car?" I chewed my lip. "And I was at Mystic Dreams checking on Angelina ..."

She shrugged, leaned down to eye level with the pumpkins on the table and squinted at them from different angles. "Unless someone came in while we were at coffee klatch."

"Tell me again why we aren't being more careful about locking up?"

Tracy opened her mouth to answer, but I said, "It was a rhetorical question, Tracy. Either way, whoever stole the holder didn't have much time to sneak in and out of here."

"Or maybe we didn't notice it missing before this morning?" She shrugged. "I guess we should be more vigilant since something fishy is going on." Tracy grabbed a pumpkin from another table, eyed the two pumpkins sitting side by side, shook her head and returned it. She skipped over to the bowl at the counter and scraped the remaining batter into the molds. "I'm pretty sure they stole it today. I would have noticed if it was gone yesterday."

She probably would have. Me? I tended not to notice things like that. Now if a tablespoon of sugar was missing from a recipe ...

I opened the front door of Confections and peered down Worth Avenue in both directions to make sure Peter was gone. It would be just like him to mosey in at a moment's notice. No one but a woman in a peaches-and-cream outfit strolled past. I stepped back inside, shut the door, and headed to the back room. On the way, I checked Tracy's work.

"Good job filling the molds only halfway," I said.

"Last time the batter dripped all over the oven."

Yup. I opened the door to the back room.

A note in the center of my desk practically hit me in the face.

In boldface letters: **Stop looking for the thief.**

CHAPTER THIRTEEN

I called the police right away and waited in the café. A few minutes later, an officer patrolling the area arrived and asked me the typical questions: how long was the back office unattended, was anyone else in Confections with us that gained access to the back, like that. I told him the only ones so far had been me, Tracy, and Peter, and that Peter only came in to the front and only stayed a short while. The officer asked if maybe Peter could have gone out the front door and come in through the back. I told him it was possible, but I had never seen him do anything criminal, only disgustingly hurtful, in our years together. The officer looked at me with surprise and a little bit of pity.

"Did I say that out loud?" I asked. "I'm fine. I'm over it ... him. I'm over him," I said with great confidence. "Hey, does this mean we get police protection now that we've graduated from criminal mischief?"

"You want personal police protection?" he asked, amazed.

"Well, yeah."

Tracy sat at a café table petting Sweet Pea, and nodded her head vigorously.

I exchanged glances with her. "I don't feel exactly safe here."

He placed the note into an evidence bag, sealed it, and mumbled to himself, "I hope they can get some fingerprints this time."

"What do you mean?" The officer shook his head in a dismissive gesture, scribbled something on his notepad and said, "Detective Trumble will come by to ask more questions."

"Trumble? Why? He only deals with murder."

"That so?" The officer smirked.

The front door flew open. Trumble, wearing a pink Tommy Bahama shirt and dangling a lollipop stick from his mouth, marched over, petted Sweet Pea as she ran up to greet him, and looked at the officer. "What do we have?"

The officer produced the evidence bag, the two had a short discussion, and the officer left with the bag.

Trumble asked me the same questions the officer had, only in more detail. Twenty minutes later, he stuck another Tootsie Pop in his mouth and shot out the door.

Neither the officer nor Trumble clued me in to what they were thinking. My nerves were shot. I heaved a big sigh, grabbed a glass of ice water, and joined my two best friends in Palm Beach aside from Aunt Mary—Tracy and Sweet Pea—at a table.

Tracy asked, "The police still can't put anyone on alert here?"

I nodded and gulped half my water. "Seems like it."

"We're supposed to wait here like sitting ducks for the next bad thing to happen?"

I nodded my head up and down like a dashboard bobble doll. "Yup." Then, "No. You know what? *No.*"

Tracy twirled a pumpkin by the stem. "Oh, no. What are you going to do?"

"Never mind. Let's get the day started," I said and jumped to my feet. "Hopefully we'll have customers to pet and feed all day. And espresso-needing owners."

At my heels, Tracy asked, "Don't you think it's time to add a biscotti or something?"

"One of these days," I answered, my mind on other things.

Tracy stopped at a pumpkin. "Mind if I do something with these?"

"Be my guest."

A woman wearing a Lilly Pulitzer dress and holding a dog leash with a beagle at the end peered inside the display window. I waved her and her pooch inside. The rest of the day was uneventful, aside from a dachshund and a Pomeranian having a conversation that ended with both owners scooping their dogs into their arms.

Sweet Pea and I skedaddled home at the end of the day. I fed her, showered quickly, and spent a full half-hour on my makeup. Sweet Pea eyed me from the bed with eyelids half-shut while I brushed my hair up into a ponytail and let it loose about five times.

"Why do I bother?" I said aloud. I leaned down, plumped up a pillow and said, "Wish me luck."

Her ears twitched and her eyes opened slightly wider to confirm she wasn't coming with me.

"I promise I'll be back before you know it."

Ten minutes later, I drove up the long, elegant entrance to The Breakers, the infamous oceanfront luxury hotel. A valet scurried to the driver's side of my car, and I stepped out, feeling all fancy in my high heels and little black dress. I dashed inside, trying not to break my neck in the black pumps I hardly ever wore anymore. Immediately, my eyes scanned the Italian Renaissance-style architecture and décor.

I strolled over to the super-sized vase of flowers. "Gorgeous," I said aloud.

From behind me, "Yes, you are."

I turned from the vase and met Peter's gaze.

He lightly grabbed my elbow and led me into a massive marble hallway. "The beach and pools are this way," he murmured into my ear.

"They don't allow access unless we're hotel guests."

Peter smiled that half-grin. "What's the worst that can happen? They tell us to come back into the hotel?"

And then we get to be embarrassed. Why would we put ourselves into that position?

"I don't think so," I said. "Let's just go into the lounge." I shook my arm loose from him and strode back up the hall the way we had come, fully in control of myself and the situation when *wham* ... the heel of my pump broke and I almost fell flat onto the cold, marble floor. Luckily, I only slammed into the wall.

"Sam!" Peter called. "Are you alright?" He grabbed my arm and held it firmly.

My face felt hot. I chewed my bottom lip and hobbled over to retrieve the broken heel lying in the middle of the hall. "I'm fine." I took both shoes off to inspect the problem. "It looks like the glue came off. I haven't worn them in a while. I guess the Florida humidity didn't do them any favors."

"What do you want to do?" he asked.

"About what? These?" I asked and raised my shoes in the air. I looked at them and made the executive decision to break the other heel off so at least I could walk without bobbing up and down between steps, then slid them back on my feet. "I'm game if you are."

We strolled past the front desks to the cocktail lounge, where I did my best impression of someone who wasn't humiliated. I smiled, relaxed my shoulders, and even laughed at Peter's lame attempts at humor. In the lounge, the soft music from a jazz band created the perfect backdrop to the sparkling jewels and colorful attire of the crowd. On my one trip to New York City, everyone had seemed to wear black. Not so here in South Florida.

Peter and I sat in plush chairs and ordered drinks. He pulled out his wallet and grinned. "Just to show you that I won't make you foot the bill this time."

"Where did you find it?" I asked.

"I'm an idiot. It must have fallen out of my pocket near that flower shop in your courtyard. Somebody nice left it for me to find on the table near those gigantic pumpkins. They didn't even swipe my cash."

"You found it at Frederika's?" Where Dominique had purchased the pumpkin. "And whoever picked it up didn't steal your money?"

"You guys still having trouble with people stealing stuff around here?"

Had I mentioned that to him?

"As a matter of fact, one of my napkin holders is missing."

The waiter set our drinks down and asked if we wanted an appetizer. Peter looked at me, and I shook my head no. I needed to make this evening as short as possible before his charms wooed me back into a relationship where he broke my heart … again.

I lifted my glass and sipped my martini.

"You sure you don't want something more exciting?" he asked. "They have all kinds of fancy drinks here." His eyes scanned the men and women, so unlike the people in our little town of Sun Haven. His eyes sparkled as he checked everybody out.

"I like martinis."

"They suit you." He met my gaze and quietly said, "Classy."

"Okay, now I know you're up to something. Can we just be real here for a minute, Peter? Stop the fake charm act?"

"It's not fa…" He must have noticed my stern face because he straightened up in his chair and changed topics. "Tell me about this stolen napkin holder."

"Not much to tell. I had a napkin holder. It got stolen."

"Are you sure it didn't get broken and someone just threw it out?"

Hmmm. A furry wiggly-worm is the most likely culprit. The owner could have been too embarrassed to admit it.

"I guess that's possible," I said. "I didn't think of that."

"See?" he asked. "I can be handy to have around."

I was enjoying playing the game with Peter, but the part I don't like is where it ends up with him winning me back and me walking in on him with another woman. "Somebody left a note on my desk."

"What kind of note?"

"A warning to stop looking for the thief."

"How does someone know you're looking?"

"Because my reputation precedes me, I guess. The last time we had trouble on Worth Avenue, I sort of let my impatience get the best of me and almost got killed by the murderer."

"What?" he asked, astonished.

"Yeah. I know. But the police are so slow."

"That Dominique woman was only killed a few days ago, wasn't she?"

The scent of the stuffed mushrooms at the table next to ours made me a little queasy when I pictured Dominique lying on Patisserie's floor. "I just wish they had brought the murderer in already."

A young woman strolled past and glanced at Peter, who pretended not to notice. Her dress draped her body in that ultra-casual but sophisticated way that screamed, "I'm so rich, I can throw on anything in my closet and it'll look fabulous."

Peter said, "Life here is a lot more exciting than Sun Haven."

I drew up my eyebrows.

"I just mean, all this talk of murder, thieves, and death threats." He gulped his gin and tonic and eyed a man wearing shiny shoes and a thousand-dollar suit. "Do people meet here for business meetings, you think?"

"I'm not sure. Why? You thinking of drumming up business for your windsurfing company?" *Oh, God. He's not really thinking of moving here, right?*

"Pretty sure I can't afford the rent in this town," he said, all smiles. "Unless you let me move into your aunt's estate?"

"You heard I live on Aunt Mary's estate, huh?"

"Could be cozy, the two of us in your cottage ..." He leaned in close enough that I could smell his musky cologne.

I breathed in his scent, then snapped back to reality. "Wait. I didn't tell you I lived in a cottage on her estate. How do you know all of this?" *So that's it. He wants to move to Palm Beach to step up the ladder in life, make more money.*

Peter leaned back in his chair but fixed his eyes on mine. "All kidding aside, I know you can be impatient. But do me a favor and be careful. If someone left a note, it means this is serious. They're trying to scare you off, which means you should be scared. Stop looking for the thief and let the police handle it."

I held his gaze, my mind zipping around all the angles of his words.

"If someone was listening to you right now," I said, "you're warning me away because *you* wrote the note."

He laughed that away with the ease of someone who has nothing to worry about.

We spent the remainder of the evening enjoying the music and catching up. But the worries never completely left my mind and by the time we were through, I was ready to go home to the safety of my cottage and my dog and get some answers.

As Peter and I meandered out to the front of The Breakers and waited for the valet to retrieve our cars, he leaned over, kissed my cheek, and said, "It's still early ..."

The valet scooted over with a smile. *Saved by the valet ...*

"Goodnight, Peter." I dashed into my car and on to Whitehall. Once there, I opened the electronic gate, peeked up at the dark windows in the Big House, and parked in front of the cottage. Soon as I opened the door, Sweet Pea greeted me with sleepy eyes and a wagging tail. I threw out my broken shoes, slipped on a pair of sneakers, and walked her around the grounds on a leash to keep her safe should a raccoon or opossum show up. Then we returned to the cottage, where I showered and settled on the couch with my laptop.

The responding officer that day had mentioned something about fingerprints. I thought about who had complained of stolen items: Angelina, Jenny and Dominique.

I scooted myself backwards on the couch, laid one hand on Sweet Pea's fuzzy back and used the other to click links about what kind of person is apt to steal. The internet was alive with more than enough information. Too much, in fact. People who suffer from OCD or kleptomania who can't seem to fight the inner urge. Or who feel a thrill from stealing a bar of soap from a drugstore. Or enjoy the rush of a hammering heart as they snatch a woman's purse.

Next, I looked up reasons people might get blisters. This list was even more exhaustive. Everything from allergic reactions to medicines, food poisoning to sports injuries. I rubbed Sweet Pea and narrowed my focus: Dominique had blisters and was stabbed. I found no correlation between stabbing and blisters. Big surprise.

I couldn't see a connection between the blisters and stabbing. Even the blisters on Dominique's mouth and fingers were probably unrelated. She had probably played too many sets of tennis and maybe ate a mango, which I knew from experience can cause latex-fruit syndrome and make the lips swell.

"What about the stomachache?" I asked out loud.

Sweet Pea lifted her head. Tucked it back down.

I typed in "stomachache and blisters" and once again the internet offered more information than my brain could digest. Any number of things can cause this. Usually, an allergic reaction. Had Dominique been on any medications? I had no idea.

My cell rang on the end table. I picked up.

Bethany said, "When I got into my car after work tonight, somebody in a hat and coat was watching me. I called out hello, but they strode off. Remember Dominique said she saw someone in a jacket and hat watching her on Worth when she was jogging?"

"She said she would do something to whoever it was before they could continue stealing."

A sudden thought exploded in my head. "The other evening some-one was watching me swim at the beach. They were gone when I tried to see who it was."

"Are you sure it wasn't just somebody who happened to be on the beach and had nothing to do with you?"

"Probably. Same goes for you, then, tonight."

We sat in silence for a moment.

I massaged Sweet Pea's ears. "Someone left a note in my back room at Confections today."

"A note?"

Something scraped loudly on the front window of my cottage. Sweet Pea jumped up and barked.

"Bethany, I have to go."

I hung up and listened for sounds outside, my heart beating in my chest like the fluttering of blackbird wings.

CHAPTER FOURTEEN

I kept my cell on me while I crept to the front window. The blinds and curtains were closed. Again, I heard a noise. Maybe a tree branch. Sweet Pea let out two quick barks.

"No one could get through the estate's privacy walls, right?"

I called Trumble.

He picked up on the third ring. "Yeah?"

"I hear somebody outside my window."

"You call 911?"

I paused. "No. My aunt has fortified walls … it's probably a tree branch … right?"

"I told you I'm not here for your personal emergency service," he grumbled from the other end of my cell.

Sweet Pea barked another piercing bark.

I peeked out the curtain to see if any lights were on at Aunt Mary's. "Can anyone get up and over the estate walls? Because I hear something outside and that along with the note makes me think it's not a tree branch."

A loud cracking sound made me cry out.

"Samantha ... Samantha ..." Trumble said from his end.

I sucked in raspy breaths, peeked out the front curtain ... "I don't know. It's definitely somebody ..."

"Hang up and call 911. I'll call Mary." He hung up before I had a chance to argue.

An hour later, after a squad car and Trumble came and left and Aunt Mary had been woken up, I felt like a first-class idiot when the officers agreed a raccoon had probably paid us a visit.

I went to bed and texted Bethany back to tell her why I had rushed off the phone.

Bethany: A raccoon?

Me: My aunt said he's been eyeing her cocktail fruit trees.

Bethany: What do you think?

Me: Beach, note, napkin holder. Something going on. Need sleep. See you at coffee klatch.

I turned out the light, and tossed and turned for three hours before I finally fell asleep.

CHAPTER FIFTEEN

M y eyes felt glued shut the next day. I pried them open with two cups of the strongest coffee I could stand and worked a crossword puzzle from my *Super Simple Crossword Puzzle Book* to relax, then walked Sweet Pea around the estate grounds instead of around the block. After the steamiest shower with the coldest rinse the tropical Florida shower pipe could provide, Sweet Pea and I made our way earlier than usual to Worth Avenue.

I slowed in front of Mystic Dreams when Angelina cowered with her arms over her head at the familiar young woman and man hovering over her. I pressed the brake and gasped when the woman slapped the shop owner. Angelina's hand shot up to her cheek.

I opened my driver's side window.

"Hey!" I yelled. All three stopped in their tracks. The woman and man turned to me and as they did, Angelina scooted inside.

The woman chased after her, tried to turn the doorknob and called, "Open the door!"

"What do you think you're doing?" I asked.

"Mind your business," the man said. His tee shirt and jeans matched the woman's style, completely unlike Angelina's flowing skirts and exotic accessories.

The man kicked Mystic Dream's front door.

"I'll call the police!" I shouted.

I checked my rearview mirror. A Mercedes behind me flashed their lights. I drove forward, parked, and ran out of the car with Sweet Pea toward Mystic Dreams. The man and woman were racing down the sidewalk. I peered inside the shop at nothing but darkness and a strand of twinkle lights. I turned the front doorknob but it was locked.

"It's Samantha, Angelina. Open the door!"

I knocked and pounded on the door. After several moments, my knuckles turned sore.

Worried about the New Age store manager, I traipsed over to Patisserie for coffee klatch and arrived at the table of women. But with all the strange happenings, I got the heebie-jeebies and just wanted to be at my own store. Right inside Patisserie's front door, Dominique had been lying dead only a few days ago ...

"Hey, guys?" I asked. "Mind if we move coffee klatch to Confections?"

"Why?" Bethany asked.

"I keep picturing Dominique on the floor inside."

"It's not like you didn't have a dead body on your floor a month ago ..."

Tracy, wide-eyed looked at me.

"Thanks, Bethany," I said. "You're always a source of comfort." We exchanged sarcastic smiles.

"Let's go, ladies," she said and gathered her belongings.

Tracy and Jenny followed her lead, and we all headed over to Confections.

"All I have is espresso and some tea bags," I said.

"Fine with me," Jenny said. She stood up, picked up her coffee cup, and began limping from the patio to the sidewalk.

"What happened to you?" I asked.

Bethany said, "Take a wild guess."

I looked at Jenny. "What did you try now?"

Jenny shrugged and tucked her surfer-girl hair behind an ear. "I had a windsurfing lesson last night."

I stopped walking and gaped. Something niggled in my brain, but I ignored it because I pictured the young woman trying to hold onto a sail with her hands while balancing on the surfboard in the waves. "Last *night*? As in when it was *dark* out?"

Bethany said, "She loves the thrill of taking chances."

Jenny stuck up for herself. "It's not like it was pitch-dark. There was moonlight."

Tracy snorted, Bethany shook her head, and Jenny simply curved her lips in a semi-smile.

We all continued on to Confections without analyzing the situation ... Jenny never failed to give us an exciting story to talk about. I wasn't as brave—or foolish—as her, even when I was her age seven years ago. Barely out of her teens, the young woman needed to do what we all did at that age: make bad choices.

"You're going to get yourself killed one of these days," I said and immediately wished I could retract my words. I turned around and glanced back at Patisserie. "It's so weird that Dominique isn't here to stop by on her morning jog, isn't it?"

The three women nodded sadly. Jenny reached into her pocket, pulled out a pack of tissues, a mini-hairbrush, a Chapstick and a pack of bubble gum, and offered me a pink rectangle. "Bubble gum always cheers me up."

I chuckled. "No kitchen sink in your pockets?"

"Huh?" she asked.

I raised my mug. "Don't want the sweetness to interfere with my bold roast."

We all walked past Bethany's art gallery. Sweet Pea barked at her reflection in the glass window.

"You'd think she would understand it's her own reflection by now," Bethany snipped.

"Leave my dog alone," I told her. To Sweet Pea, "That's only your own cute face." I felt my spirit lift. Or maybe my third cup of coffee was kicking in.

As the four of us marched over to Confections, Sweet Pea wagged her tail and padded happily alongside us. Unlike her feelings for Whitney's murderer, whom Sweet Pea had never warmed up to because she had seen her kill Whitney, my dog seemed comfortable with these women.

"Thanks for moving this to Confections," I said. "It seems like every time I leave it for too long, I get a bad surprise."

Jenny asked, "What kind of surprise?"

Tracy said, "A nasty note."

"And the overturned chairs," Bethany said.

"And the missing napkin holder," I added.

"Geez," Jenny said. "You really have had a rough time of it." She opened the front door of Confections, since my hands were full with the dog leash and my mug of coffee from home.

Once inside, I unclipped Sweet Pea's leash. The girl ran over to her water bowl.

Tracy wrapped her arm around my shoulders and squeezed. "Whoever is doing this is going to pay. I got your back, Samantha."

I chuckled lightly. "You're a good egg, Tracy Oshkosh."

Bethany said to me, "And *you* still talk like you're from the 1920s."

Jenny watched the exchange. As the new girl in town, she, along with Angelina, sometimes didn't seem to know what to make of us. Bethany didn't give her as hard a time as she had given Tracy and that she continued to give Angelina. Maybe because she sensed weakness in the two women, though I did my best to encourage Tracy to stick up for herself.

At the thought of Angelina, I couldn't help but worry. After we settled in the café, I told the others what had happened with the man and woman in front of Mystic Dreams and ended with, "I hope she's alright. Think somebody should check on her?"

Jenny said, "Who do you think they are?"

I shook my head. "I have no idea. And she gets twitchy when I ask." I peered into my empty mug. "Who's ready for an espresso or cup of tea?"

Sweet Pea understood my questioning tone as in invitation to play. She grabbed her blue ball.

Tracy threw it a few feet in the café. "I'll have an espresso."

I got up and stared out the front window at Mystic Dreams, hoping Angelina would appear.

Bethany said, "I wouldn't mind an espresso."

Since neither Tracy nor I were making a move to the espresso machine, Jenny popped up. "I'll get it."

My eyes fixed on Mystic across the street. I mumbled, "Thanks ..." Hopefully, Angelina was okay. I stared out the window but with no sign of the bohemian store manager, I sighed and sat down with the others while Jenny headed slowly to the espresso machine.

"I forgot about your hurting your leg," I said and started to jump up. "Are you okay?"

She gestured for me to sit back down. "I'm fine. Go sit."

"Yes, ma'am," I said and chuckled. Jenny sounded like Aunt Mary.

She rounded the display case to the cups and saucers. "I might have my leg looked at, but I'm sure it's fine."

"Don't go to a surgeon," Bethany called over to her. "He'll just want to operate."

"You think?" Jenny asked.

"My aunt had knee surgery a couple of months ago," I said.

"How is she doing?" Tracy asked.

"She's stubborn and impatient," I complained.

Bethany chuckled.

"I know why you're laughing and I don't think it's funny," I said to Bethany.

Tracy offered, "Bethany thinks your impatience runs in the family, and your being so set on finding Dominique's murderer and the thief is exactly something your aunt would do."

"Yeah," I said. "I think we all got that."

Bethany shrugged as if to say, "Pretty much sums it up."

Jenny returned with the espressos and joined us.

And Angelina still had not emerged from Mystic Dreams.

CHAPTER SIXTEEN

After Bethany and Jenny left to open their shops, Tracy and I cleaned up. I began a batch of carrot frosting and watched while Tracy glopped another pile of hand soap onto her hands at the sink.

"Are you trying to use up all of the soap so I have to buy that lavender blend you want?" I asked.

"No," she said, scrunching her face and scrubbing her right hand. "There's something sticky on it, and it's bugging me."

I looked down at Sweet Pea happily panting on her dog bed in the corner with her ball between her paws.

"Is it from playing with the ball?"

"No, the ball wasn't sticky." She scrubbed, rinsed, and dried her hands.

I peeked over for another gander at Mystic Dreams. I didn't like it one bit that Angelina hadn't joined us. New in town, maybe she needed us, her friends. Especially if she was going through something.

I tried to remove my worry-wart hat, remember that everybody is different, and that maybe Angelina preferred to deal with things on her own.

I finished up the frosting while Tracy worked on organizing the PawCakes and PupTarts in the display case. After half an hour, we were ready to open. I stepped over to open the front door now that we were trying to be better about locking it, while Tracy disappeared to the back office. I massaged Sweet Pea and after a full minute rub-down, opened the door to the back room with Sweet Pea at my heels. Tracy sat at my desk and wrapped a Band-Aid around her finger.

"What did you do?" I asked.

"My finger is burning."

"Did you try baking again?"

"No. Well, yes. Last night at home. But no, I didn't burn myself on anything. I'm almost positive."

"You're almost positive?" I liked Tracy a lot but her daftness sometimes made me nuts.

The bell over the front door clanged. I left Tracy in the back room to greet our first customer of the day. A standard poodle and his person, a man in a Ralph Lauren shirt and sunglasses.

"Good morning!" I called out.

Sweet Pea tentatively wagged her tail from behind the display case until I got the okay from the owner that his dog didn't mind off-the-leash Sweet Pea coming over.

"Princess likes other dogs," the man said.

"Sweet Pea, want to say hello to Princess?"

My girl padded over slowly, sniffed and stepped back. Princess lifted her snout in the air and *yipped*.

The owner frowned, puzzled.

"It's the leash, I think," I said. "If everyone was off the leash, the whole dynamic would change and they could do their doggy thing."

He nodded.

"Sweet Pea, how about you give Princess some space while I take their order?"

She peered up, wagged her tail a couple of times and moseyed over to her bed.

"Good girl, thank you."

The man ordered an ice water for himself and a PupTart for his pooch. As I handed him his order, it occurred to me that if I wanted to see my profit margins increase, I needed to stop handing out free glasses of ice water and start selling bottled water. And bottled water suited upscale Palm Beach more, anyway.

I wiped the counter free of crumbs and smiled at the poodle munching the PupTart while the owner perused his cell phone. My smile disappeared when I gazed out the window to Mystic Dreams across the street. *Why did that woman slap Angelina?*

Mr. Ralph Lauren interrupted my thoughts. "I bet you wish people would stop dying on Worth Avenue."

"Excuse me?"

He walked over and handed me a business card. "I'm Dick, from *Pulse on Palm Beach.* The mayor warned us not to go to Patisserie, apparently by the owners' request. Must be nice to have money and connections, huh?"

"So *that's* why I haven't seen any press at Patisserie like when Whitney got killed here."

Dick grinned. "But the mayor can't stop a customer from coming by the area with their dog …"

I looked at the poodle. "Is that what you're doing? Using your poodle to get a story?"

"Actually, it belongs to my girlfriend."

"It? You mean *she* belongs to your girlfriend, right?"

The reporter shrugged. "Whatever."

"No wonder she looks so uncomfortable with you," I said, miffed at his manipulation. Rather than ring Dick's neck, I sprayed Windex on the window of the display case and scrubbed it to a high gloss. "You thought you would come over here and see what information you can glean from me? I had enough of that last ti—"

Tracy suddenly appeared from the back room. "Samantha." She held up her swollen hand. "I think I need to go to the doctor."

CHAPTER SEVENTEEN

I called my aunt on the way to the hospital. She had insisted her knee felt well enough to drive and meet us in the hospital parking lot to bring Sweet Pea home while I waited in the ER for Tracy. Eight hours later, it had been determined that Tracy must have had an allergic reaction to something.

"That's all they told you?" I asked as I walked next to her wheelchair on the way to the hospital exit.

"Why do I have to be in a wheelchair?" she asked the orderly.

"We have to ensure you make it out of here safely," the man with the muscles answered.

Tracy said to me, "Sorry I made you miss the whole day at Confections."

"I'm just glad you're okay." I gestured to her bandaged hand. "Feeling better?"

"They gave me painkillers so I am for now. That was really weird. It went from burning to a blister to blowing up like a balloon. They said if I waited to get medical attention, it could have turned into something much worse."

I left her at the curb in her wheelchair and ran over for my car. I picked her up, thanked the orderly, and helped Tracy into the passenger seat. After I shut her car door, I rounded around the back of the car and slid into the driver's seat, all the while wondering what the heck was going on. "It's weird you mentioned blisters. Dominique had them, too."

I pulled out of the parking lot and headed to Tracy's house. "You'll have to leave your car on Worth Avenue tonight."

"Do they allow that?" she asked and dozed off for a moment before lifting her head off the headrest. Groggily, she said, "I think I'm okay to drive home."

"You sound like Aunt Mary telling me she could drive even when she was taking painkillers for her knee."

"Your aunt is as impatient as you are when it comes to waiting until things run their course," she said sleepily. "Except the murderer would have been running loose a few days longer if it wasn't for you putting your two cents in."

"Did the doctors mention the cause of your allergic reaction?"

The air conditioner blew Tracy's ponytail tendrils around her skinny, little face. "They asked if I ate or drank anything new lately, or touched any new plants. Even herbs can cause an allergic reaction. The only thing I did different was eat a box of candy with red dye listed as an ingredient."

"*You* ate candy?"

The girl had a personal trainer, ate yogurt for lunch, and salad for dinner. Which explains why she weighed all of maybe one hundred ten pounds.

"I know," she said. "I went to a movie at CityPlace and couldn't resist the snack counter. Do you know how bad red dye is for you?"

I glanced over at her hand and sighed deeply. By the time we reached her mansion's gate fifteen minutes from the hospital, Tracy was snoring again. I roused her from sleep to ask her the code, rang the front door, and handed her over to the house manager.

I hadn't been to Confections since earlier that day and with everything going on, I didn't feel comfortable not checking on it. I would have liked to go on home to Sweet Pea, but my aunt was nothing if not dependable. Sweet Pea was fine.

I drove to Worth Avenue for a quick look-see at Confections and spotted Angelina on the sidewalk in front of Mystic Dreams. I parked in front of my dog bakery, saw that—from the outside, at least—all looked okay inside, and ran across the street to check on the flowery woman.

"Angelina?" I called. "How are you doing?"

"Wonderful. I'm cleansing my sidewalk." She waved a handful of something in the air. Subtle bits of smoke spiraled upward.

"Cleansing it?"

"With sage."

"Does that work when you do it in the open air like this?" I looked up at the setting sun.

"It has to." She gathered herself. "I mean, of course it will work." Angelina swung her arm back and forth maniacally towards the sky.

A door slammed shut across the street at Sophisticated Pet. Rick closed his shop for the evening and even from this distance, Sexy Stubble and I locked eyes for a moment. I didn't know how to react. *Smile? When Angelina was clearly so distraught?* I turned from him and back to Angelina.

"Does this have anything to do with the man and woman who keep showing up?" I asked.

She continued to wave the sage in the air.

"Angelina?" I asked again. "I saw the woman slap you."

Her arm stopped waving for a moment, and her back stiffened. Then, she resumed her glide across the sidewalk and wave in the air.

"If someone is giving you a hard time, you should let someone know. You have friends. You have us."

She stopped then. Lowered her arm. Turned to face me, eyes shimmering. "That's very nice. But I'm afraid you can't help me." She lifted her arm again and went back to cleansing. Almost in a whisper, she said, "Frankly, it's not your business."

I felt her words as though she had slapped me in the face. Coming from her, they sounded harsh. Much harsher then if Bethany said them. I waited to see if maybe by some chance this was just fear talking and Angelina simply wanted to keep herself—or me—safe. But her face turned neutral and she set her feet back to gliding, her arm back to waving.

"Alright, then," I said. "I'm sorry to get into your business. I'll leave you alone."

She paused for a fraction of a moment, then resumed pacing.

By now, Rick had disappeared.

I climbed into my car, anxious to get home to my cottage and Sweet Pea, and said a little prayer as I drove: *Please let tomorrow be a better day.*

CHAPTER EIGHTEEN

T he next day, I held Sweet Pea while a vet tech clipped her nails, and my dog didn't even hold it against me. Afterward, she and I walked on the sidewalk on yet another sunny day in the Sunshine State. Sweet Pea's chin lifted in the air as she padded down the sidewalk, seemingly proud of the bandanna the tech had loosely tied around her neck. Orange, with black cats covering it.

Looking forward to a day of rest and relaxation, I strolled with my girl past one of the doctors' offices and ran into Jenny.

"How's your leg?" I asked while Sweet Pea greeted her with happy licks.

"It's fine. I went to the doctor for my headaches," she said and pointed at the row of offices behind her. "It's hard to keep up with my ailments, I know."

We walked in step, with the Florida sun shining broiling overhead as if it were August instead of October.

"You ever think about stopping your daredevil activities at least until you get all healed up?"

Her hair lay on her shoulders like yellow fluff. Not unlike Peter's. He had been texting me nonstop since our drinks at The Breakers.

She didn't answer, only shrugged, so I asked, "Do you have time for a Starbucks? It isn't autumn unless we have a pumpkin latte."

"Sure, why not?"

We headed over to the courtyard at CityPlace, the shopping, entertainment and dining district in West Palm Beach. Walking past the Diva Duck truck, I asked, "Have you ever gone on that? It's really cool. It drives you to the water and then turns into a boat, and you can see all of the mansions."

"Like your aunt's?" Jenny leaned down to pet Sweet Pea as we walked.

"No, you can't see hers from the boat tour. You should come over sometime," I said. "I have a cute cottage my aunt lets me live in."

"For helping her with her knee, right?"

Jenny, like the other women, were privy to most everything, thanks to coffee klatch-ing for the past month.

"She doesn't let me do much. She's stupid-stubborn about hurrying things along."

We ordered our Starbucks and sat outside, chatting and observing the shoppers walk past with their purchases.

Jenny said, "If I can manage to keep my job at Patisserie, maybe I'll be able to afford to go shopping here."

"It's not as though the prices here are the same as on Worth Avenue." I paused and sipped my coffee. "And what do you mean, manage to keep your job?"

She shrugged. "In case you haven't noticed, I haven't had too many customers since Dominique was killed."

"I know the feeling. It's the same at Confections."

She peered up through pale, blonde lashes.

"It'll get better once things die down," I said with more confidence than I felt.

"You think?" she asked.

I thought about Canine Confections not exactly getting on its feet yet. "Absolutely." Then, "I'm almost sure of it."

For the next few minutes, we sat and sipped and petted Sweet Pea along with any other dog that came within petting distance. After a cocker spaniel stopped by for a quick pat on the head, Sweet Pea reached up and licked Jenny on the arm.

"Yuck!" Jenny said, laughing. "You got my arm wet!"

"Sorry," I laughed. "She tends to do that to people she feels comfortable with."

Jenny rubbed my girl's fluffy head. "They also pick up on their owner's energy."

"You sound like Angelina."

"How is she?" Jenny asked. "Does anybody know?"

I thought about my last encounter with her but didn't want to repeat it. It felt somehow disloyal and gossipy.

Three chihuahuas on leashes yapped as they passed us in the court-yard. Sweet Pea stood up and stared. The owner shouted over their yaps, "Sorry! They like your dog!"

"You sure about that?" I asked. One of the chihuahuas growled at Sweet Pea, who stuck her tail between her legs and whined softly at my knees.

Jenny's cell rang. She spoke loudly to be heard above the dogs. "I'm fine!" she yelled into the sudden quiet now that the dogs had passed. She ended the call. "Ever miss the days when you could hang up on someone instead of press End?"

"You mean you remember land lines? What were you, two years old?"

"I'm only a little younger than you." Jenny stared down at her cof-fee cup. "That was my mother. She worries too much."

"Don't they all? Mine only gives me a break because she knows my aunt is here to keep an eye on me."

She removed the plastic lid from her cup and fiddled with it. "She said I shouldn't be working so hard and stressing myself out, espe-cially after my surfing accident. If the migraines continue, she'll bring me home."

"She can't bring you home. You're twenty years old."

Her face grew sullen. "What she means is, she'll cut me off. She and my father are paying my bills. Rent, food, electricity."

"Oh." I thought about it. "But Patisserie pays you."

"Not enough to pay the first and last month rent in my rental house in West Palm plus the car I had to get and to fix it … it's expensive being an adult."

"You're telling me." Sometimes I forgot how good I had it living on Aunt Mary's estate.

"They want me to make something of myself and to give it a go on my own, but when they see me get the least bit stressed, they threaten to bring me home like I'm a child." She stood up and shook her hands like they were full of bugs. "Feel like walking?"

"Sure."

Sweet Pea and I got up from Starbucks and strolled around CityPlace—past the specialty cheese store, the bottom of the escalator leading up to the comedy club and movie theatre …

We wound around the corner and came upon The Cheesecake Factory, where Angelina and the two people I kept seeing at Mystic Dreams exited. Angelina didn't see us. She didn't look too happy, but she didn't look upset, either. Then, right there on the sunny sidewalk in front of the passersby and the others exiting the restaurant, the young woman shoved Angelina slightly. Not much, but enough that Angelina looked at her with a hurt expression.

"Did you see that?" Jenny whispered, incredulous.

"Yeah. I know."

Jenny started to head over. I latched onto her arm gently. "I've already talked to her about it. She doesn't want us involved."

"You've talked to her?"

"She said it was none of my business."

Jenny made a face. "Well, I hope she's at least planning to give that girl a problem right back." When I responded with a raise of my eyebrows, she chuckled and said, "Comes from years of chest noogies from my brothers."

Angelina and the two people disappeared around the corner. Jenny, Sweet Pea, and I strolled past a tequila bar. Jenny tugged on my arm.

"Yeah, I don't think so," I said and laughed.

"Give me one reason why not."

"I have to drive home. And Sweet Pea is with me. And it's the middle of the day. There. That's three reasons."

"Don't tell me you're one of those people that only drinks a margarita when you eat a Mexican dinner."

I nodded. "Afraid so. I'm more of a hot chocolate with marshmallows kind of girl."

Jenny left me and Sweet Pea on the sidewalk as she slipped inside the tequila bar and returned two minutes later with a salt-rimmed margarita. "Want a taste?"

"They let you take alcohol in a to-go cup?"

She shrugged and grinned.

I frowned at her. "Won't that make your headache worse?"

She laughed. "Are you kidding? It'll make me forget I even *have* a migraine."

Before too long, Jenny started chatting more than a junior high school girl trying to win over a clique of friends.

"... and then," she said, "I snuck into my brother's bedroom and tore all the heads off his G.I. Joes."

"That's ... extremely terrifying."

Jenny laughed at me and shrugged. "He deserved it. I loved my Ken doll, and he tore off his legs."

"It sounds like your family has anger issues," I said. "Geez."

"You know who needs to get some fire in her belly?" Jenny asked.

When I glanced at her with an inquiring-minds-want-to-know eyebrow raise, she answered, "Angelina. How can she let that girl shove her like that?"

"I know." I broke down and told Jenny what I had seen the day before, ending with, "But she told me it was none of my business, so I guess I have to stay out of it."

We paused at the Restoration Hardware display window and stared at the crystal cabinet knobs.

Jenny licked the salt off the rim with the childlike glee of Tracy.

"You know ..." I bit my lip, not sure how to approach it. "I notice there's a little ... tension ... between you and Tracy."

"She's jealous."

"Of you?"

Jenny shook her head. "Of me with you. What do you have in common with her? But you and I ..." She gently tapped my shoulder with the arm holding the margarita and sloshed a little onto my bright yellow cotton top. "... we sell sweet treats."

"Don't forget we both found a dead body on our shop floors," I added. Like with Whitney, Dominique's death didn't feel real.

Jenny's face fell. A pallor changed it from suntanned to white.

"I'm sorry to come out and say it like that," I said. "Sometimes it all seems like it's just a dream or a movie or something. I can't believe it actually happened … two murders on one little strip of Worth Avenue."

Jenny threw out her cup. Tears coursed down her cheeks. She began, to my utter surprise, blubbering and wailing, going on about the horror of it all, finding Dominique's body, not knowing what to do, screaming, waiting for 911, answering Trumble's questions …

When her rambling subsided, I said, "I know. I'm so sorry."

Shoppers walked past, glancing awkwardly at Jenny, then at me. Sweet Pea wagged her tail slightly in the same tentative, nervous gesture she does when something is wrong and she doesn't know what to do about it.

I pulled a pack of tissues out of my purse and handed them to Jenny, trying to pull her into an alcove and away from the crowded sidewalk. When at last she quieted her tears and seemed to have no more to say, she blew her nose and wiped her face.

She stared down at her feet. "It happens every time."

"What happens?"

"When I drink."

"You had one drink."

She threw out her tissue in the nearest trash receptacle and tried to laugh it off, but her chuckle sounded more like a croak. "My mouth opens and doesn't stop until everything in me pours out in a weepy torrent of emotion." Still feeling the effects, I'd guess, she went on. "Ever since the surfing accident."

"What do you mean? From the concussion?"

"Yeah. I mean, mostly it's just the migraines. But things like this, alcohol affecting me. I didn't used to be such a lightweight." She didn't stumble or wobble, but her eyes didn't look quite as clear as usual.

"I think I had better drive you home."

"I can drive myself."

Another one who thought she could drive herself.

She stumbled and fell into me and Sweet Pea.

I grabbed her arm. "Your car will be safe in the parking garage. I'll bring you back to get it tomorrow." I guided her and Sweet Pea towards the garage. The three of us piled into my car and, thankfully, Jenny was sober enough to at least tell me where she lived. We pulled up fifteen minutes later to a modest house. Sweet Pea and I followed her up the walkway from behind to make sure she got in to her front door without falling. I had planned to return to my car and finish out my day snuggled with Sweet Pea in my cottage watching a movie, an ocean swim later in the afternoon, and an evening of puzzles with Aunt Mary … assuming she wasn't baking pies with Mr. Lollipop.

Jenny struggled to insert the key into the front door lock. I reached over and slid it in, and turned the knob, then stepped back.

Jenny said, "Come on in."

"I need to get home."

"Oh, come on. You've never been here. See what you think of the place."

I stepped inside. Sweet Pea padded in, tongue lolling.

"Does she need water?" Jenny asked.

"That'd be great, thanks. You don't have cats or anything, right?"

"Cats? No. Why, does she not like cats?"

"I don't know. I've never seen her with one."

I unhooked Sweet Pea's leash and let her roam free while Jenny disappeared into another room. Sweet Pea stayed with me and stuck her nose to the floor and sniffed. "Excellent field work," I teased her.

Jenny called from another room. "I'm in here."

I followed Sweet Pea into the kitchen. Jenny pulled out a bright, red apple from a bowl on the counter and chomped into it. "Want one?" she asked and pointed at the bowls of fresh fruit.

"I guess drinking doesn't give you a headache and nausea?"

"Huh? No, I'm good. Let me show you my backyard," she said and tripped over the threshold.

"Maybe you should sit down until the margarita wears off."

"Let me just show you … it has a patio set and umbrella that I love to sit under in the evenings after I get home from Patisserie."

She didn't have a tennis court, cocktail fruit trees with lemons, limes, and oranges, or a pool like Aunt Mary. But she did have a concrete slab, a tree with little green apples, and a birdbath. I didn't want to show my surprise that parents from upscale Lake Worth—whose close friends hired their daughter a job managing their pastry shop—paid only for a rental house more fitting for someone of—let's face it—*my* economic stature.

Out of nowhere, Jenny vomited in a rose bush.

If there's one thing I can't stand, it's watching someone throw up. I turned away. After a quick glance at Jenny to make sure she was alright, I grabbed Sweet Pea's collar and led her inside while I looked for a garbage pail even though it was clearly too late.

I left Sweet Pea inside, returned to the yard, and steered my eyes clear of the rose bush. Sweet Pea panted and stared at me through the sliding glass doors.

Jenny said, "That was gross."

"You're telling me. Is that from one drink?"

"I haven't eaten all day except for that bite of apple."

We headed inside the house and she disappeared into the small bathroom off the short hallway.

"Are you on any medications or anything?" I called through the door.

Through the bathroom door, I heard the faucet running and Jenny gargling.

The water shut off. She opened the door. "The migraine pills."

"Maybe you shouldn't mix it anymore."

She nodded and led me to the couch.

I started to join her, but my cell rang.

From the other end of my cell Tracy said, "Want to come over and watch a movie or something? I'm still feeling weird after the hospital."

I looked at Jenny, curled up on the corner of her couch hugging a pillow. "Sure," I said into the phone and hung up. "You going to be okay?" I asked Jenny.

"I'll be fine. I think I have some ginger ale in the pantry." She perked up and played with the pillow in her lap. "Hey, want to watch a movie? We can order pizza later. It'll be fun."

"That sounds good, but that was Tracy. She still isn't feeling well and wants company."

I looked at the girl who also seemed to want my company and couldn't help but feel guilty. But I couldn't invite her to Tracy's. I had never been there myself yet.

Jenny got a faraway look in her eye for a second, and it occurred to me that she, like I had been a couple of months ago, was new in town and didn't have many—or any—friends. *It's too bad Angelina is so secretive. Maybe she and Jenny would be good for each other.*

I said, "How about tomorrow when we pick up your car at the garage, we make a day of it? Lunch and a movie at CityPlace, or if you like the beach, we can go to the dog beach with Sweet Pea."

She returned my smile with one of her own and ran a hand through her sun-bleached hair. "Sure. I wonder if we should invite Angelina? The more, the merrier, right?"

Thank goodness Jenny was open to embracing Angelina.

The New Age store manager looked like she could use some good friends.

CHAPTER NINETEEN

My least favorite part of running a dog bakery is that I have to get up at four a.m. Not the fact that I get up ... the fact that I *have* to. I do not like being told what to do. I'm like a teenager that way.

Therefore, I was none too thrilled when three hours later, after coffee klatch at Confections, Trumble told me to have patience with all the cases of criminal mischief on Worth Avenue, that he was working a murder investigation. He was a little snippy about it, too.

Coffee klatch had ended abruptly when the detective showed without prior notice. Jenny softened it by inviting everyone to Patisserie for fresh guava pastry. Bethany, of course, declined due to using up her daily allotment of fat in her Starbucks cappuccino. Jenny looked a little disappointed but perked up when Angelina and Tracy followed her out the door.

In Confections' café, Trumble sucked on his lollipop while I stood behind the display case with a mixing bowl and beaters. I broke out in a whine. I'm not proud of it, but enough was enough. I complained about my overturned chairs, missing napkin holder, and the warning note. I finished with, "Since criminal mischief means most of what's going on around here won't even get into a police report, do you think there's a chance that you're missing out on valuable information?"

He scowled. "Like what?"

"I don't know. That's sort of my point. Maybe you're missing something."

His scathing look said it all. "Pretty sure we got it covered."

"And I'm pretty scared." I met his stare, then plastered my eyes to the bowl and beaters, wishing that my most pressing concern was coming up with a new recipe. I finally found my voice. "The last time I was too afraid to tell you everything, I almost got me and Sweet Pea hurt."

"I never told you to egg a murderer on."

"But she was just running loose out here!"

"Be careful this time." I took that as a sign that I could snoop around and see who might be performing "criminal mischief." I would let the professionals find out who murdered Dominique.

Trumble left Confections as Donna from *Pulse on Palm Beach* shoved the door inward. The reporter loved the drama and limelight, and hadn't taken no for an answer when she had wanted the inside scoop on Whitney's death. Needless to say, she wasn't on top of my Most Wanted list right now.

"I told your buddy Dick not to bother coming around," I said to the reporter.

Sweet Pea padded up to her, sniffed and licked, then curled up on her bed behind the display case.

"He told me."

"Then what are you doing here?"

"Can't blame a girl for trying."

"Yeah, actually. I can."

She chortled like this was all in good fun. "I just want to see how all of the shopkeepers are faring with another murder. Especially you. This makes two for you."

"Only one in my shop. And it's not like I killed Whitney."

"No. And Jenny probably didn't kill Dominique, either. That's why it's so remarkably sad that you two have to go through this." She peeked over her shoulder at the still empty Worth Avenue sidewalk. "Here you are, trying to get your business going, and life just won't give you a break." She drew a pen out of her purse and held it atop a notepad like I would start gabbing and provide her with a story.

"We're fine on our end of Worth Avenue," I said.

Again, she peered over her shoulder at the empty sidewalk, turned back to me, and raised her brows.

I insisted, "It's still early in the morning. We'll be fine."

She grinned and scribbled in her pad. The more I tried to convince her that all of our businesses on our little strip of Worth were fine, the more she smiled and scribbled.

Tracy skipped in the front door with a box of guava pastries.

"Oh, right," Donna said to her. "I forgot you work here now."

I had hired Tracy from *Pulse* after she realized the paper wasn't a good fit for her.

Tracy's face fell. Donna marched out the door with a smarmy smile.

"Don't let her bother you." I opened the pastry box. "These look amazing."

"They are," she said, licking her fingers. "I already ate one. Help yourself."

Sweet Pea appeared, wagging her tail and staring up pitifully at us.

"Can I?" Tracy asked.

"She gets enough treats."

"Sorry, Sweet Pea. Your mom is very mean."

I pulled out a pastry, then bit into it. The fruit and light texture of the puff pastry tasted like a tropical island and Paris at the same time. "This is delicious."

"I know. Angelina and Bethany missed out."

"I thought Angelina was going over there with you guys."

"Do you know Jenny gave me a plate for my pastry even though I'm not an official customer? I think she misses having coffee klatch. Why did we move that over here again?"

"Tracy, I asked you about Angelina. I thought she was going over to Patisserie with you guys."

"She was, but then she got a text and ran over to Mystic."

I finished my pastry and washed my hands in the small sink behind the display case. I moseyed to the front door to make sure all looked okay at Mystic and to check if any customers might be coming our way. Or maybe even Sexy Stubble. *Though Rick seems to have better things to do than come by and say hello to me.*

I opened the front door, peeked down Worth Avenue in both directions, and saw someone slip into Rare Books and Stamps, a very rare occurrence.

"I'm a little worried about her."

"Who?" Tracy asked. "Angelina?"

"Yeah."

"Why?"

"I don't know who those two people are that come around, but she seems pretty upset by them." Turning back to my own business, I surveyed the tables, chairs, benches, and bench cushions in the café. "We need more napkins."

Tracy said, "And I guess we have to buy another napkin holder to replace the one that got stolen. I'll go to the back and get some more napkins," she said, her hands dripping water from washing them.

"I got it," I said and shoved open the door between the front and back of Confections. The exit door to the patio stood ajar. I peered out at the patio table where I often ate lunch in the peace and quiet of the courtyard.

There on the table, sat the missing napkin holder.

CHAPTER TWENTY

As my stomach plunged into a sickening spin at the napkin holder and what its return implied, my cell rang.

"Samantha!"

"Mom? Since when do you call me in the middle of the day? Are you and Daddy alright?"

"Yes, I'm sorry. I didn't mean to scare you."

I sat at the table and stared at the napkin holder. Something told me not to touch it. If the beat cop decided he had time to check the fingerprints, I didn't want to mess them up.

"Mom, I have to get back into the bakery ..."

"How is Canine Confections going?"

My parents had missed my grand opening because they had purchased non-refundable cruise tickets before the whirl of my move to Palm Beach. They had come up from Sun Haven once so far, which was fine by me. Let at least a month go by without a dead body before they visited. I didn't want to tell her that business hadn't exactly been booming, not that I knew exactly where Confections' numbers were in the plus and minus columns. *Maybe I should stop avoiding it and check the books.*

"Is it too late to move home to my old room and live with you and Dad?" I asked, only half kidding. "I'll share it with your craft supplies." In the back of my mind, I found comfort that I could always move back home with my parents. So many twenty-somethings were doing it nowadays.

She said, "Don't be silly, my daughter, the entrepreneur." Then, "Guess what. Your father and I have sold the house and are moving into a retirement community!"

"What?"

"It will be so much easier for us. We won't have to mow our own lawn or rake our own leaves."

"Florida doesn't get leaves in autumn."

"Of course it does. And you know what I mean ... we can take it easy. We've been working so hard all our lives and with you gone, we can finally relax."

"Thanks a lot."

"Oh, honey, I didn't mean it like that."

I sat on the patio bench and concentrated on a ladybug on one of my potted plants. "You and Daddy aren't old enough to retire. How can you move into a retirement community?"

"We're not retiring. We'll still work. But we only have to be fifty to live there, and we reached that milestone a couple of years ago. We're lucky we got in. The apartment rentals are sky high here in Sun Haven. You could never afford it on the salary you were earning at Debbie's Bakery. I'm so glad you moved in with Aunt Mary."

Huh ...

My parents were moving out of my childhood home.

My mother went on. "I just wanted you to be the first to know. I'm going to call Mary and tell her now."

My mother hung up. I stared at my cell. Then the napkin holder. Then my cell again.

Tracy burst out of Confections' back door. Before I knew it, she grabbed the napkin holder and squealed with delight.

"Where did you find it?" she asked and turned it over and over like it was Harry's Sorcerer's Stone.

"No!" I yelled, too late. Her fingerprints were all over it.

Tracy dropped the napkin holder to the concrete. It broke into pieces. She bent down to pick them up.

"Stop!" I said.

She snapped her head up at me.

"I don't want you to cut yourself. Plus, the police might be able to get fingerprints from it." Shards lay everywhere. "Or not."

"Oh." She looked crestfallen.

"It's not a big deal. They probably wouldn't have gotten much anyway. And that's assuming they would have bothered coming. A

returned napkin holder doesn't even fall under criminal mischief."
Though if this wasn't mischief, I didn't know what was.

"I better get this cleaned up before someone gets cut," I said and headed in the back door.

Tracy, at my heels, said, "You're not even going to bother trying to get fingerprints off it?"

I grabbed the broom and dustpan and held my knee in front of Sweet Pea's furry muzzle. "You have to wait in here until we pick up all the ceramic pieces, little girl." To Tracy, "I guess I can call the police and see what they have to say."

We began to clean up. I admonished Tracy for starting to pick them up with her bare hands, like she was my daughter instead of my best friend.

After we got it cleaned up, we returned inside. I called the police who, no surprise, didn't have time to check into a napkin holder that had been returned.

I set to work on a bowl of cupcake batter to get my mind off of everything. The napkin holder, the phone call—realizing I had nowhere to go as a self-respecting twenty-seven-year-old who already took my Aunt Mary's last dime ... unknowingly, but still ...

A man entered the front door of Confections without a dog. "Where was the dead body lying?"

I stopped stirring the batter. "Excuse me?"

"The dead body," he said gruffly. He wore a sleeveless tee and jeans, and I knew right away he wasn't a resident of Palm Beach. His hair didn't have one dollop of mousse or gel.

"That was a month ago," I answered.

"It was just the other day," he said and slid a chair over to lean his foot on while he tied his shoe.

"You're getting my chair dirty. And I think I can remember when a dead body was found in my own shop."

"Oh!" Tracy said with a big grin. "You're thinking of the dead body a couple stores over!"

The man and I stared at her. Her enthusiasm surprised me less and less.

He dropped his foot to the floor. I ran over and wiped the chair clean.

"Is that the bakery with the dead body?" he asked.

Tracy announced proudly, "Yes. *Patisserie of Palm Beach.*" She led the way and pointed out the door two stores to our right.

He left without a thank you.

As Tracy bopped back inside, she yelled, "Ouch!"

I turned from my bowl of batter. "What's wrong?"

Sweet Pea walked over to her and sniffed.

"Nothing," Tracy said, holding her hands in the air. "It's just ... my fingers ..."

"You touched the broken napkin holder?"

She shrugged. "Just a small piece." She wiggled her fingers. "I'm okay."

Tracy helped me finish my batter by grating fresh carrots into the bowl as I stirred.

"Ooh, let's add raisins!" she said.

"Nope."

"Why not?"

"Grapes are toxic to dogs." I leaned over and kissed the top of Sweet Pea's furry head.

The front door swung open but rather than a paying customer, Bethany sauntered inside. "Hey, girls," she called out.

"Hi, Bethany," we said in unison and continued finishing up the carrot cupcakes.

"Just thought you might want to know," she said. "Rick just told me the dog dish at his store was returned."

I stopped stirring and left it for Tracy. "I didn't know he had a missing dog dish. How would he even notice one missing dish?"

"Doing his job taking inventory?" Miss Snippy retorted.

"And it was missing, you say?"

"Yes," Bethany said, exasperated. "But like I said, it was returned."

As much as I wanted to know the goods on Rick, the dog dish interested me more.

"What happened?"

Bethany sat in the café. "What happened what?"

"The dog dish?"

"I told you. It was returned."

"Yeah. I got that. When? Where? How?"

She stood up again. "I don't know. If I thought I was going to get the third degree I would have asked more questions."

"So, nothing then? It was stolen, and it showed back up?"

"That's all he knows, that's all I know." She gestured with her chin back at Tracy before leaving. "What's wrong with Little Miss Muffet?" she asked on her way out the door.

I turned around to see Tracy in front of the mixing bowl holding her hands in the air with fingers splayed.

"What's wrong?"

"I don't know," she said. "They feel weird again. Like burning or something."

I grabbed some ice. "Here. See if this helps." I sat her down in the café. "I don't see any cuts. Did you burn them in the oven again this morning?"

She held the ice to her hands. "I don't think so. Oh, you know what? How about we try a sweet potato recipe? I saw a can of solid sweet potato when I was at Rick's looking for something to buy Sweet Pea the other day, and I figured why not just bake something with a fresh sweet potato?"

I had already thought of this, but I didn't want to douse her enthusiasm. "That sounds like a fabulous idea. Let's create a doggy sweet potato recipe. What do you think? Pie or cookies or muffins or just sweet potato bites?"

She shot out of her chair, threw the ice in the sink and checked her phone. "Ooh, I don't know. Let's see what we can find online."

"Or we can create our own," I said.

Her finger issue forgotten, Tracy got lost in her phone, which left me free to move forward. Rick's dog dish and our napkin holder showing up were not a coincidence. I wanted to do some research again, but first I needed to see if things were as bad as I thought with our finances.

"Trace, do a Buy One Get One Free thing today for anyone who comes in. Let's see if we can generate some energy here."

She nodded and set her phone down, then raced over to the drawer behind the display case and pulled out some magic markers. "I'll make a sign, with lots of colors. And sparkles to draw in the eye and add excitement."

I laughed. "Sounds good." And better than the kindergartner sign I would have come up with.

"Sweet Pea, want to help me?"

My fuzzy girl followed me to the back room and investigated the shelves, back door, and walk-in closet and refrigerator while I opened my online books and checked our numbers. As I suspected, Canine Confections wasn't making a profit, not that I needed my books to tell me. All I had to do was look out into the café and see the empty chairs. Aside from our canceled first grand opening, looky-loos without dogs interested in the murder site, *Pulse on Palm Beach* trying to keep the story alive, and now another murder two shops over, I couldn't imagine the problem. And besides all of that, a thief was stealing and sometimes returning items. "No problem at all, folks, nothing to see here."

Sweet Pea blinked up at me.

"We have to go home later and make sure Aunt Mary is doing okay with money. Okay?"

The girl lolled her tongue. I smiled back.

I wouldn't be smiling for long at what I found when I got home to Aunt Mary at the Big House.

CHAPTER TWENTY-ONE

After a cocktail hour with Pellegrino on ice and a fresh chunk of mango from the tree in the backyard, Aunt Mary, Sweet Pea, and I settled into the cozy kitchen nook and enjoyed a meal consisting of simple fare.

"This is different for Chef Luca," I said and took a bite of fresh spinach salad.

"I made this," Aunt Mary said.

"You? With your knee?"

"No. With my hands." She smiled and forked a bite of salad into her mouth.

"You know what I mean. You're not supposed to stand for too long."

Sweet Pea, not very interested in the scent of our vegetable salad, soup, and crusty French bread, laid her chin on her front paws and chuffed.

"Why didn't Chef Luca prepare dinner?"

She waved her fork. "He only comes three times a week. This isn't unusual."

"I know, but normally we eat what he prepared. Aunt Mary, what are you not telling me?"

I hadn't yet told her about our numbers, thinking the sweetness of the fresh strawberry shortcake during dessert would counteract the sour news.

"I let Chef Luca go," she said uneasily.

"Why? Did he do something?" *Please let him have done something and not let this be about money.*

She avoided my stare. "It's not as if I'm not capable of cooking my own meals. If I hadn't married Uncle Joseph, I'm sure I would have been cooking all of these years."

But Uncle Joseph was gone now, and Aunt Mary had lived her entire adult life as a woman in want of nothing.

"Your investment in Confections ... it's worse than we thought?"

She laid her fork on her plate. "Matthew said if we don't see a profit, I could lose Whitehall sooner than we anticipated."

"Your financial advisor said that?"

She quickly glanced at something on the counter. I followed her line of vision and marched over to a basket of pamphlets. *Sunny Isles. Caribbean Dreams.*

"Aunt Mary, these are living communities."

She wiped her mouth. "I thought we had a little more time to get Canine Confections off the ground. But it's okay."

"How do you figure?"

"Matthew said as long as Confections begins to bring in any kind of profit now, I won't have to move out of my home."

Fabulous.

CHAPTER TWENTY-TWO

T he next morning, I woke up at two a.m. I had barely slept all night. I kept falling back asleep and dreaming that Chef Luca was chasing me with a cleaver and trying to chop off my fingers. The last time I woke up, I laid in bed wiggling my fingers like Tracy had been doing the day before.

My eyes half-closed, I turned on the coffee pot and walked around the gigantic yard with Sweet Pea. Not the entire yard but enough that she did her business and we both got a little exercise.

"I owe you a long walk around the block or on the beach, little girl," I said.

She padded happily at my side as we traipsed through the fruit tree section of Aunt Mary's yard. If my aunt had to give up her estate because of Confections, I would never forgive myself, and I mean never. It simply wasn't an option.

As we rounded the cocktail tree, something white and furry raced past. Sweet Pea took off but listened to me when I called her name.

"Good girl!"

Her ears flattened back a bit. She loved being called a good girl.

"Who was that?"

I walked hesitantly toward the spot where I had seen the small animal, not at all sure I wanted Sweet Pea involved. A squirrel would just race up a tree. But someone else? "Hello?"

Nothing.

"Well, it wasn't a raccoon," I said to Sweet Pea. "They aren't white." We searched around the fruit trees, the tennis court, circled the pool a couple of times, but there was no sign. "There is no such thing as a white squirrel, right?"

Sweet Pea panted her reply.

We returned to the cottage. I fed my girl her breakfast, and sat with my coffee and computer looking up things like, "How to get your business going when there's been a dead body or two in your neighborhood." Most of my clicks led to True Crime stories.

I poured another mug of coffee, added a dollop of whipped cream for the pure comforting pleasure, and said, "Just for the heck of it, let me see what happens when I type *Dominique* and *stealing* in a Google search."

Nothing turned up. I tried to squash the feeling of disappointment that rose in my throat. *What did I expect? A big, splashy photo of Dominique with an arrow pointing to her head that said THIEF?*

Rather than type in every person I knew and the word *stealing*, I concentrated on the website links that popped up with information aplenty on the different types of thievery. *Who knew there were such varying degrees?* A burglary is if someone breaks into a house. If somebody breaks into a home and steals something, it's a robbery. Then there's theft. And if someone steals something and brings it back? That could simply be someone playing a trick.

After showering and piling myself and Sweet Pea into my car for work at 3:30 a.m. to see if I happened to run into the same person Dominique had told us about, I heaved a sigh. I had forgotten my purse. On my way to the cottage, I tripped on a tree branch. Then I dropped my key and kneeled in the grass for a full minute before finding it.

I finally managed to get everything I needed and drove us to Confections. After settling Sweet Pea in and refreshing her water bowl, I secured both the front and back door locks to ensure she was safely inside, and left in search of Dominique's wanderer who, for all I knew, was simply someone out for a morning stroll.

To my surprise, quite a few people were strolling about at four in the morning on Worth Avenue and the alleyways.

"This is strange," I said to myself. "Why are there so many people? Dominique made it sound like there was one person scampering around." Perhaps I had put too much trust in the woman I had only known through our coffee klatch visits?

With no shady-looking folks to spy on, I turned the corner to the courtyard where more shops and the patios for Patisserie, Bebe, and Confections lay. Lo and behold, a figure wearing a coat, hat, and gloves moseyed about. Even with the slight chill in the air in the middle of the autumn night, Florida rarely warranted this type of attire. The brim of their hat covered their forehead and part of their nose. No telling if it was a man, woman, or mongoose.

I tiptoed behind them for five full minutes, creeping into a corner when they paused. For all I knew, they were out for a normal walk, but if so, they had a funny way of doing it. Stopping at store windows, standing and staring at other people across the courtyard.

At one point, they must have felt my presence behind them because they wheeled around. Panicked, I nonchalantly traced my hand on a store window as though I were out strolling the courtyard same as them. Beyond the window, my fingers caressed a bucket of dead flowers that Frederika the florist had thrown next to her shop.

A few moments later, my back to the coat-clad person, I heard footsteps behind me. They were coming more quickly, and for some reason, an army of goosebumps danced up my spine. I peeked over my shoulder as though I would find a monster staring me in the face instead of a human being, but when I turned around, no one was there.

I called out to the empty, dark patios, "Wait!" but heard no response.

On my way to the patio of Confections, I ran into a palm tree on Patisserie's back patio.

"Ouch!" I yelled.

Frederika and Jenny sprang out of their patio doors.

"Are you alright?" Frederika asked, a bouquet of orange carnations in her hand.

"Just clumsy," I said and tried to smile.

She returned back inside her flower shop.

Jenny smiled at me. "You okay?" With only the light from Patisserie's back room, I barely made out the outline of her surfer-girl body.

"Half asleep but yeah. I didn't realize so many people were out at this time of morning."

"It's a little early for a florist to be working, but in the bakery business, it's a given to be up at dawn, right?"

"I guess. This is a little early even for me."

"Want to come in? I just took some peach tarts out of the oven."

"Is that what I smell?"

Like a puppy to a bone, I followed the sweet scent in to Patisserie's back door and up to the front café. Jenny slid a chopping block with freshly-sliced strawberries off to the side and removed gloves similar to the ones I wear when I slice jalapeños.

"Those look like really good quality," I said and gestured to her gloves. "I wonder how much Angelina spends on accessories?"

Jenny laughed. "She never seems to be without a scarf or hat or gloves, does she?"

"Some people have a knack for style."

"Not me. I'm happiest in a bathing suit and shorts."

She sounded like Peter. I reached over and idly twirled one of the lemons in a bowl. "My aunt has fruit trees all over her yard. I love it."

Jenny plated my tart and grabbed the bowls of lemons, limes and green apples, then placed them on the back counter. "I love having fresh fruit around." She held up the tray of peach tarts. "Now all I need is a peach tree on my patio. I had to bake these with peaches from Publix."

I bit into the warm tart. "Nothing wrong with the local grocery store if your tarts come out this good."

"I think I'll make another run. I wonder what time they open?"

I shrugged and chewed, immersed in the sweet goodness in my mouth.

"What's the news on you and Peter?" Jenny asked as she wiped off the counter.

I threw her a dirty look and forked another bite of tart into my mouth.

She laughed. "That bad, huh?"

When I didn't answer with anything more than a nod, she said, "Say what you want about your old boyfriend, but he is one good-looking dude."

I sighed resignedly, swallowed, and found my voice. "That's what people keep saying, but it's more than that. He's also too charming for his own good. Or for my own good, I should say."

Jenny sat and gazed out the window at Worth Avenue. "Plus, he has that whole surfer look. Lean, sun-bleached hair ..."

I laughed. "Like looking in a mirror, huh?"

She chuckled and ran a hand through her shiny mane. "I better brush this back before I open or the Goodwins will have a conniption that I don't fit in here."

I had been so caught up in my morning investigation, peach tart, and Peter that I forgot I had been standing in the exact spot Dominique had been a week ago.

Jenny said, "Tell me the truth. You were out here trying to find out who Dominique was talking about." She stared at me and waited.

"What if I was?"

"Detective Trumble might have an issue with you trying to involve yourself again. Didn't you say that he was finding out who killed Whitney and there was no need for you to put yourself in danger?"

"He wasn't finding out fast enough."

She laughed. "Peter is right."

"About what?"

"About you. He said you're impatient to the point where if a duck didn't swim fast enough you would help him flap his wings."

"Ducks swim with their feet."

She snickered. "Whatever."

"When did you see Peter?"

"He came by looking for you."

"Where?"

"Here."

"In Patisserie?" I asked. "Why would he look for me here?"

She shrugged and fiddled with a napkin. "He probably knew we used to do coffee klatch here."

"He came one morning?"

She turned her face from mine. "No. One afternoon."

"Okay, then he didn't think I would be here for coffee klatch."

My old boyfriend was making the moves on Jenny. *Some things never change.*

Jenny got up. "I think he was fishing."

I sighed and got out of my seat, ready to go back to Confections and continue the day that had started so well.

"I'm sure he was," I said. "I mean, look at you. You belong on the cover of *Beach and Swimwear.*"

"Is that a real magazine?" Then, moving on, she shook her head. "I think he was fishing for information on you. He wanted to know if you were dating anyone. Like that."

"What did you tell him?"

Rick had hardly been around lately, except for the times I had run into him while with Peter. And the time I saw the woman with his same good looks acting friendly and familiar outside of Sophisticated Pet.

"I told him he should ask you," Jenny said.

Tracy may be the best friend I had in town, but I was hoping Jenny would continue to become a part of my new circle of friends.

We said good-bye as Jenny grabbed her keys for a quick run to Publix. For the moment, I set aside my hopes for a deeper friendship with her. Something told me that I couldn't trust everything she said. Did Peter really come by? Or did she seek *him* out? Not certain if it was my trust issues thanks to Peter and Claire, or if I truly had something to worry about, I texted Tracy to see if she could come to work early since Sweet Pea was there by herself, and followed Jenny's car in my own.

The beach goddess didn't head to Publix for peaches. While it was possible that she had innocent errands to run, I didn't think it likely when she pulled into a parking spot in front of the medical buildings where I had been with Sweet Pea the other day. Did she have something to hide? Why wouldn't she simply tell me that she had a doctor's appointment?

Perhaps I was being too hard on her.

Or maybe it was Peter who still didn't deserve my trust.

CHAPTER TWENTY-THREE

T he sun had risen on the drive over so I waited in my car under a palm tree from a safe enough distance that Jenny wouldn't notice me.

She disappeared around the corner of the office building, so I quickly exited my car and followed her from thirty steps behind. After she opened and shut a door, I skedaddled up to read the plaque: Jeffrey Ugums. Psychiatry.

I didn't want to jump to conclusions, but we did find a dead body on her bakery floor. She told me she was here the other day for a doctor's visit for her headaches. *Had she lied? And if so, why?*

I checked the time on my cell and searched the area. A juice shop stood a few doors down. Also, a Tarot Reading shop and a café. I could pretend I decided to get my tea leaves read and eat breakfast and that I happened to run into her.

And she would never buy it.

I hemmed and hawed and made my way back to my car. I didn't know what was going on with Jenny, and I was pretty sure Peter hadn't killed Dominique, if only because I didn't want to think that I was attracted to a murderer. Surely there were other suspects?

I slumped into the front seat of my car and blasted the air conditioning into my face. Sweet Pea was still at Confections, but I had locked her securely inside. No one was getting in. Plus, Tracy had said she'd rush over.

With Sweet Pea safe, I let my mind wander to my next moves. First, I would find out more on Jenny, though if the poor girl was simply seeing a mental health professional, there was no shame in that. I very much wanted to call Detective Trumble and ask him for an update on with the investigation, but he pretty much never answered my inquiries when I asked.

I angled the vents so the cool air hit my face. I would make my next move later that night. Scoot around Worth Avenue and, this time, I wouldn't do it in early morning or broad daylight. I would hide behind a planter if I had to in the dead of night. If someone shady was wandering around, I wanted to know about it.

I laid my head back on the seat rest, closed my eyes, and breathed in and out slowly as if I were meditating.

Three loud knocks next to my left ear made me jump so high that my head hit the ceiling above the steering wheel. My hand flew to the top of my scalp. I rubbed it as if it would ease the pain, then turned and gaped at Jenny, glaring in through the driver's side window.

I tore my eyes from hers and slowly opened the car door, though I remained seated behind the wheel. "Hey! Look who it is."

We met each other's gaze.

"Don't even try it," she said.

CHAPTER TWENTY-FOUR

I waited in my driver's seat so I would have an escape route if Jenny lashed out at me. Since we were in the middle of a sunny street, I didn't think she would dare.

After a moment, when her body language suggested curiosity more than irritation, I exited my car, holding my gaze steadily on her.

"I was following you," I admitted.

"No kidding." She looked ... hurt.

"Sorry. I had a feeling you were lying about Peter."

Her jaw dropped, but I kept going. "I thought maybe you two had started seeing each other after I gave him the cold shoulder."

"And what? You thought I was meeting him for a secret morning coffee rendezvous?"

"Are you?"

"You know I'm here at the psychiatrist's office."

I didn't pretend to be surprised.

"And no, I'm not crazy," she said.

"I never thought—"

"Yeah, you did. I could see it all over your face." She stepped out into the street.

An older couple in Palm Beach pastels shuffled past. After they were down half a block, I said, "I'm not so stupid that I think going to a psychiatrist means you're crazy."

A car horn beeped at Jenny, half out in the street.

"Would you come up onto the sidewalk please?" I asked.

"Why?" She waved her arms at her sides. "I can do what I want."

"Get over here!" I said and reached out to grab her.

She yanked her arm from me. "Ever since I moved here … 'Watch your back, Jenny! Toe the line! Wear your hair tucked behind your ear!' It's like one wrong move and I'll lose everything … my job as the manager at *Patisserie*, all of you as my friends, my own rental house …"

Yelling now, and closer to the middle of Royal Palm Way, Jenny didn't budge as a car zipped past and blared its horn.

"You're going to get hurt," I pleaded. "Come to the sidewalk."

At that time of morning, traffic was slow, but even so I couldn't help but worry.

"Jenny, please …"

She cast her eyes to the pavement and, after a moment, stepped over to me.

Her voice barely above a whisper, she said, "She was just lying there on the floor." A tear fell from her eye.

"Who? Dominique?"

Jenny nodded and wouldn't look up.

"I know how hard that must have been for you."

She peered up through wet eyelashes. "How did you get over it?"

Taken aback, I said, "Get over it? You mean Whitney?" I thought about that. "I don't know that I have."

"I keep imagining her with the knife stuck in her." Tears poured down her cheeks now. "I never thought it would look like that."

I opened my car door and retrieved a packet of tissues.

"Thanks," she said, drying her face. After a minute, she said, "I'm going to the psychiatrist because I'm having a hard time getting over finding Dominique."

"It's only been a few days ..."

Another elderly couple passed, this one with palm fronds dotting their clothes. The man nodded at us in a gentlemanly way and lifted his hat from his balding head.

Jenny and I stared in a shop window for a minute.

"I really scared you going into the street," she said with a little smile. "That's what you get for spying on me."

"Sorry about that. Peter makes me a little nuts. One of many reasons I need to stay away from him."

After a few minutes, Jenny and I said good-bye and I plopped into my car. I was angry with myself. Angry for running around like a chicken on a busy road chasing her. Angry for following every innocuous lead as though I knew what I was doing ...

... and angry because Jenny made me see that I was a shallow, unfeeling person who had almost forgotten the horror of finding a dead body on my floor only one month earlier.

CHAPTER TWENTY-FIVE

On my way to Confections after leaving Jenny, I thought about how maybe she wasn't the only person who was affected by seeing Dominique on Patisserie's floor.

I parked my car on Worth Avenue, smiled at Tracy inside Confections throwing the ball for Sweet Pea before we opened, and examined the front of Mystic Dreams. Through the sheer front window curtains, Angelina sashayed doing who knew what. Watering a plant, maybe. I crossed Worth and dashed through the alley next to the New Age shop. I turned the knob to the shop's back patio door, let myself in and prayed that Angelina hadn't yet installed security cameras like we had discussed at one of our recent coffee klatches. If she found out I was spying while checking her camera footage, she would never forgive me.

Thankfully, Angelina didn't hear me due to the flute and harp music blaring overhead. She danced around the room, waving a cluster of sage as she smudged the room. On the face of it, she seemed to be floating in a meditative calm. But I observed her more closely. Her jaw was set, her eyes blazed. On a table set against the wall, her plant collection had grown. I didn't know their names, but I recognized one with large leaves and spikes … aloe, the plant with the sticky goo that heals sunburns maybe …

Something that Tracy had told me bubbled beneath the surface of my brain.

Quietly, I stayed to the shadows and tiptoed to the front room, trying not to sneeze from the musky scent of the sage. I felt a sneeze coming on. Before I sneezed and signaled to the *second* friend that day that I was spying, I dashed back out the door to Mystic Dream's patio, then rounded the building toward the front of the store.

Angelina's voice called from behind. "Who is that? Come back!"

I switched from a jog to a fast run up to Worth Avenue. If Angelina had simply stepped outside her front door rather than run after her intruder—me—out the back door, she would have found me gasping for air with a guilty look on my face. I darted across Worth Avenue before she caught up to me, and grabbed the gold doorknob on Confections' front door. I twisted the knob and …

… panicked when it didn't turn.

"*Now* Tracy remembers to keep it locked." One glance over my shoulder told me I had better get a move on. Angelina rounded her building in an attempt to find the interloper.

I ran to my left, through the narrow alley between Confections and Gallery Bebe, and rushed through the patio door to my back office.

Tracy, having heard the back door slam, appeared from the front, Sweet Pea at her heels.

My dog whined a happy hello and ran over to me, tail wagging side to side.

"Hi, little girl," I gasped. Sweat poured down my face and neck. To Tracy, "Didn't you see me try to open the front door?"

"We were playing ball." A small smile spread on her pixie face. "What are you doing?"

"Nothing."

She shrugged slightly and a gleam shone in her eyes. "Okay."

She may make me nuts because of her daffy, silly ways, but when it came down to it, she was a nice person. And really, was anything more important than that? I pictured Tracy, Jenny, Bethany and myself becoming and remaining steadfast friends. And just because I didn't fully understand Angelina's ways—or her smudge stick dances—didn't mean she wouldn't also be in my circle of friends.

Tracy, Sweet Pea, and I moseyed out to the front to open up.

I unlocked the door to find Angelina across Worth Avenue in front of Mystic Dreams with the same young woman and man I had seen so many times before.

CHAPTER TWENTY-SIX

A ngelina is starting to fray. This thought came to me as I watched her interact with the two people in front of her store. I couldn't understand why she spoke to them out front, for all the world—all of Worth Avenue, at any rate—to see, especially when they seemed to upset her so much. They always seemed to show around the same time, either in the early morning or in the evening at closing time.

"Do you think we should call the police?" I asked Tracy.

She joined me at the window.

"Think the police would care about people coming to her store?" Tracy answered. "They would probably say she should be grateful for their business."

"They never buy anything. She doesn't even let them inside."

"Yeah. That's weird."

"I'm worried," I said. "Look at her."

Even from Confections' café, Angelina's hair resembled the nest of newborn baby birds, her clothes didn't match, and her belt hung loose. In her shop, she'd looked swept up, fanciful. I hadn't even noticed her mismatched shoes.

Tracy opened the verticals on the front window a little wider, her fingers slightly pink.

"Your fingers okay?"

She wiggled them. "Yeah. Why?"

"Weren't they burning or something the other day? And now they look a little pink."

She shrugged. "They're okay, I guess."

I steadied my gaze on Tracy steadying *her* gaze on Angelina and her two visitors.

Deep in silence inside my cozy dog bakery, I snapped to attention when the front door flew open. Peter strode in with one red rose and a sideways smile.

Sweet Pea started to pad over and I thought maybe she would lick him hello for the first time, but she instead, she walked to Tracy. I squinted at my furry dog when I remembered that the only person she wouldn't lick was the person who killed Whitney. Probably, my dog got a bad vibe from Peter and that was all there was to it.

"Where did you come from?" I asked Peter. He had seemed to appear out of nowhere.

He pointed in the direction of Patisserie and Gallery Bebe.

Across Worth Avenue, Angelina's visitors began shouting, though I couldn't hear what they were saying from inside Confections. Angelina simply hung her head.

Peter handed me the rose. His cell rang. He dipped into his jeans pocket, pulled out his phone, and shoved it back in. Then, he beamed at me with those stupid green eyes of his. He tucked a stray strand of beachy hair behind his ear. I wanted to ask who had called, who he ignored, just like he had done to me during our last few months together. But I stopped myself because doing that would open things up too much. He would know I still cared, and I wasn't quite ready to show him. In fact, I didn't know if I *did* care.

Tracy tore her eyes from Mystic Dreams and watched us with an amused smile. *Happy to entertain*, I wanted to tell her.

A customer and a beagle entered the café.

I said to Peter, "I need to get to work."

Tracy led the customer to the display case, and I overheard her announce it was Buy One Get One Free.

"I'll leave but, in case you're wondering, that was a woman I dated a few times that I don't want to talk to," Peter said.

"Why would I be wondering?"

He lightly grabbed my arm. Out of earshot of Tracy and the customer, he said, "I know what I used to do to you was wrong. I've changed."

"And since I didn't assume that was a woman but thought maybe it was just a sales call, now I know you were avoiding another woman. You did the same thing to me. How is that changing?"

His face morphed from suntan to light red. "She was treating me like crap. Telling me she was done with her old boyfriend, and then I catch them together at Lucky Lou's."

I knew Lucky's well. It was a favorite among the twenty-something crowd back in Sun Haven.

"So you're just getting back at her," I said. "That's what this is with me."

I grabbed him lightly by the arm and escorted him to the front door.

"She wanted me back before I came here to see you. I was just explaining why I didn't answer her call. And I told you about it. Doesn't that count for something?"

"Yeah. It means you're still playing games. Call me when you grow up." I opened the door. "Or better yet, don't."

The customer and his beagle headed to us at the door. I stepped aside so they could get by.

The man asked, "Was the dead body over there by the counter?"

I bit my lip. "Yes. But Whitney got killed a month ago. It's very sad, but we're trying to put it past us."

"A month? I thought it only happened a few days ago?"

Again, we had been confused with dead Dominique at *Patisserie*.

"Is that why you came in?" I asked.

The man looked at me, looked at his beagle, and shrugged. "I'm a fan of ghost sightings," he said and left.

Still standing at the door with Peter, I was in no mood for his she-nanigans. "Why don't you just go, Peter?"

"You're clearly not ready to give this a shot."

"You're quick." It suddenly became very clear why Peter had returned. He was using me to get back at his latest conquest. Or maybe he honestly missed me. But it wouldn't last. As soon as he knew he had me, the thrill of the chase would be gone.

He stepped out to the sidewalk and shot me a look I knew well. Peeved that he hadn't gotten his way, that he couldn't win me over with his supposed charms.

I shut the door and said to Tracy, "Hopefully he'll crawl back under his rock and leave me alone."

CHAPTER TWENTY-SEVEN

T he next morning, Aunt Mary, Sweet Pea, and I sat on the patio overlooking the large built-in pool with our coffee. Aunt Mary had woken at the crack of dawn, and I wagered I knew the reason.

"Aunt Mary, I'll do something to pick my business up so you don't lose your estate."

She flashed her eyes at me. "I'm so angry with myself. How could I be so stupid? Letting your uncle be 'the man' and acting like women don't deal with finances. And now look at my predicament."

I chewed the inside of my mouth. We had been through this. Silly me, I had thought we would be free of murders and money troubles, and fall into a happy rhythm, homicide-free.

Sweet Pea held the blue ball in her mouth, inviting me to throw it. I grasped it, still in her mouth, and she released her grip. I threw it as far as I could. We watched it fly and land under an orange tree. The girl sped after it.

"It's not going to solve anything to beat yourself up," I told my aunt. "If you do that, I'm going to beat myself up for not micromanaging the situation by asking you more questions about your finances when you gave me the money."

She smiled. "You treated me with respect not asking about my finances." Her smile faded. "I feel like such a dolt."

Sweet Pea returned, panting, the ball in her mouth.

"You're not a dolt. We need to figure this out."

She sipped her coffee from a delicate cup. "Do you have any idea why people are staying away from Canine Confections?"

"It looked like we were getting things going a couple weeks after Whitney died, but now with Dominique getting killed, we're back to square one. And this time, I'm not sure the murder will fade so quickly since it's the second one in a month. It doesn't help that Dominique got killed two doors down from Confections, and people are confused about where the most recent murder happened."

"How inconsiderate of Dominique."

I felt my face flush. "Sorry. That sounded cold, didn't it?"

Sweet Pea dropped her ball and scooted her head under my aunt's chair to chase a lizard.

"I'm afraid Confections is becoming more of a paranormal attraction than a dog bakery," I said.

"This is the right time of year for it."

"Oh, right. Halloween is coming up." Peering around my aunt's giant backyard, I thought it could make a great haunted attraction with the proper staging, tunnels, lights and props. "I don't suppose you get trick-or-treaters around this neighborhood?"

"Sometimes the children buzz the front gate. I like to keep candy on hand just in case, but often, by the time I walk up to it from the house, they lose patience and are gone."

"That's what you get for living on a palatial estate."

The patio table squeaked when Sweet Pea shot under it for the lizard.

"I think he got away," I told her. My girl wasn't much of a hunter. To Aunt Mary, "A guy came in to Confections yesterday asking about ghosts." I gulped a mouthful of coffee. "No offense to New Age stores, but it doesn't help that Angelina's store is across the street." If people came to Confections looking for spirits instead of dog cupcakes, I would be out of business before I could say *bankrupt*.

Aunt Mary set her cup on the delicate white saucer with the pink flowers. "I haven't seen her store yet."

"It's not her store. She only manages it."

"Angelina is such a pretty name."

I nodded. "Pretty woman, too." Her long, wavy hair and fancy gloves were the opposite of my straight hair and accessory-free hands.

Aunt Mary lifted her cup to her mouth and before drinking said, "I have to face the fact that unless Confections can make a profit in the next month, I better sell Whitehall before I have it taken from me. If that happens, I'll have no money left to move into *any* place."

"In the next month?" I hadn't realized how dire things were. "Geez. You know, as I've said before, we can always sell Confections, and you won't lose your home."

With an adamant, firm tone that I had only heard once or twice in my life from her, she said, "No. I am not backing out on you or our deal, or the deal we made with Gabriella."

"Gabriella is the realtor. She'll find someone else to rent out the commercial space."

"And all the equipment we invested in? The walk-in refrigerator? Professional-grade mixer?"

"We can sell it," I said.

"I said no," she said. And *that* was *that*.

I inhaled deeply, trying to think of a way out of the predicament and knowing the only way out was through action. Finding the thief and murderer would be a good start.

Sweet Pea scurried under a bougainvillea. "Sweet Pea, get out of there!" I ran over and gently pushed her away from the flowery bush with the sharp thorns, and toward a harmless banana tree.

Sweet Pea took off past the banana tree toward the lemon tree.

"Where are you going?" I called after her.

A flash of white shot under the tree. I jumped up from my chair and spilled my coffee all over my tangerine slacks.

"A cat," I shouted. "Sweet Pea, come back! Don't hurt him!"

Aunt Mary stood up, and the sixty-nine-year-old woman who I thought of as one of the most elegant, ladylike, sophisticated women I knew, thrust her fingers into her mouth and blew hard in a loud whistle, then sat back down.

Immediately, Sweet Pea stopped and turned around. The cat peeked out from behind the tree.

"Who taught you to whistle like that?" It occurred to me there were many things about my aunt I didn't know. I didn't have time to ponder however, because I had no idea if Sweet Pea would try and hurt the cat.

The cat opened his eyes wide and blinked at the three of us. Frozen in place, Sweet Pea stood and stared, like the cat was a mirage. Nothing on my dog moved, not her fuzzy head, not her spindly legs, not her long, straight tail.

The cat slowly took a step closer. Stared at Sweet Pea. Sweet Pea whined softly.

"Don't hurt her," I said to my girl.

The cat, maybe seven pounds—I had no idea, never having owned a cat before—stepped closer, keeping her eyes on my thirty-five-pound dog. A moment later, after sussing out the situation, the feline strutted right past Sweet Pea, who stuck her muzzle down to the hairy white cat as she passed. The snooty creature lifted one big paw and swiped at my girl's face. Sweet Pea stepped back and cried. The cat triumphantly slinked past and jumped up into Aunt Mary's lap.

I ran over to check Sweet Pea, whose feelings seemed to be a little hurt, but whose muzzle didn't have a scratch.

Aunt Mary sat stroking the new friend in her lap.

I told her, "I think you just adopted a cat."

CHAPTER TWENTY-EIGHT

I set aside how we would navigate a cat on the estate and in Aunt Mary's mansion, more worried about Sweet Pea's welfare than the cat's, since it seemed apparent who would be in charge. Sweet Pea would be living with me in our cottage but there would be plenty of occasions when she and I would spend time in the mansion. *Hopefully, Sweet Pea will keep her distance and the cat won't turn out to be a bully.*

After changing into clean slacks, Sweet Pea and I zoomed along Ocean Avenue while I made up my mind to hurry things along to find Dominique's murderer. Even if it meant the wrath of Detective Trumble and whoever else had something to say about me inserting myself into the situation. I ticked things off in my head of how I would proceed.

Sweet Pea and I joined the coffee klatch crew already chatting it up and drinking coffee in Confections. Jenny gathered espressos and ice waters behind the display case, and Tracy and Angelina were laying the cups and glasses on the table. Bethany sat like a queen.

We hadn't met for coffee klatch the day before because I had been following Jenny to—as it turned out—her psychiatrist's appointment. Which left Tracy to run coffee klatch at Confections. And Tracy, God love her, wasn't great at running things. She was good at being sweet and nice and making things pretty.

"Here you go," Jenny said and handed Tracy a glass.

Tracy sipped what appeared to be iced espresso.

"That looks delicious. Make me one?" I asked Jenny.

"Sure!" She darted around behind the display case. Two minutes later, she set it in front of me.

"Where were you guys yesterday?" Angelina asked. "I had the weirdest thing happen, and you all weren't even around to talk about it." She swept a stray hair out of her eyes.

She still isn't looking too good. She was acting jittery and frazzled. Her hands were trembling. Her lower lip, too.

"What happened?" Tracy asked.

Angelina exclaimed, "I could have sworn somebody was in my store. But when I ran out the back to find them, they were gone."

That would be me.

Tracy coughed. I willed her to keep quiet in case she remembered my urgent entrance through the back door.

Jenny gasped. "Who do you think it was?"

Bethany offered, in her trademark sarcastic tone, "Maybe it was a ghost."

Angelina's gaze dropped to the cup of tea in front of her that smelled of the minty herbs she kept at Mystic Dreams.

"That reminds me of a guy that came in yesterday," I said, happy to change the subject. "I thought business was picking up, but he was only interested in ghosts."

"What did you tell him?" Angelina asked.

"She told him the ghost sighting was two doors down at Patisserie," Tracy said.

"I did not!"

Tracy grinned. "Okay." She giggled and rubbed her fingers. "Samantha didn't say that."

Ignoring her, I said, "I'm afraid having two murders so close together is putting my business underwater before I even got it started. And yes, I realize how obnoxious and selfish it sounds that I'm worried about my business more than poor Dominique."

Bethany said, "I hear ya. I could use some foot traffic at the gallery."

The five of us sat in silence. Sweet Pea strolled over and lay down at my feet with a heavy sigh. She didn't seem to have an answer either.

Finally, Tracy said, "My grandma used to say, 'If you sit and complain without doing anything about it, it's like you're making the choice for nothing to change.'"

A short laugh sounded from Bethany's Chanel Red lips.

I scowled at her. "Well, *I* think Tracy just gave us words of wisdom."

Tracy beamed.

Jenny smiled a small smile.

And Angelina got twitchy, flicking imaginary dust off her flowing dress with her fingerless gloves.

Tracy added, "And my *grandpa* said, 'If someone spits in your face, you spit right back.'"

"Your grandparents sound like quite a pair," I said. "I know it stinks that Dominique was killed, but is it possible the murderer had a good reason for killing her?"

Every single one of them—Bethany, Tracy, Jenny, and Angelina—looked at me in amazement. Sweet Pea was the only one who didn't judge.

"I know how that sounds," I said. "It's just … we don't know both sides of the story."

Bethany said, "You should have been a lawyer."

"Or a saint," Angelina offered.

Bethany barked out a laugh. "Samantha is *not* a saint."

After a few more minutes of Bethany snipping, Jenny serving, and Angelina staring into space with her head in the clouds, coffee klatch ended and everybody left except for me, Sweet Pea, and Tracy.

Tracy started to mix the icing for the Tail Waggin' Delights while I stood next to her at the counter and tried to remember the checklist I had begun to formulate in the car to find the murderer and save my dog bakery. Before I had a chance to make much headway, Tracy cried out. "My hands!"

I stopped mixing and looked down at her hands.

Her fingers were covered in blisters.

CHAPTER TWENTY-NINE

"D id they just pop up?" I hadn't noticed them when she served the ice water to Angelina.

"They were sore but not like this!"

She held her hands out and cried.

"Oh my God," I said. I took in a deep breath. I would be no help to Tracy if I panicked. I erased the image in my head of Tracy lying on the floor as the next victim. I attributed Dominique's blisters to tennis, but this was too strange to ignore.

I couldn't leave Sweet Pea in Confections even for a short time. Who knew if someone would break in and hurt her? I also couldn't leave her in the hospital parking lot.

Think, Samantha, *think ...*

My heart pounded. Tracy paced back and forth in front of the display case holding her hands out and shaking them. "They hurt!" She cried and said, "I have to go to the doctor."

I inhaled and exhaled. Gathered my thoughts.

"No. You need to go to the hospital." *For the second time in a week.*

I clicked Sweet Pea's leash on her, gathered my purse and led everybody out to the car.

The entire way to the hospital, Tracy cried and held her hands like they were on fire.

"Are they getting worse?"

"Yes," she said in the passenger seat, a crack in her voice.

"We're almost there," I said in as calm a voice as I could muster. My heart thudded in my chest. *This was no oven burn.*

CHAPTER THIRTY

I pulled up to the Emergency entrance and helped Tracy out. A hospital staffer ran over, asked why we were there, and frowned when Tracy held out her blistered hands.

"I'll wait for you right here," I said.

I found a parking spot close to the entrance, checked my hideaway spot for the extra key, and left the car running with the doors locked and air conditioning at maximum output. Sweet Pea settled herself in the backseat and started snoring. I pulled out my phone and googled blisters and their causes. The internet brought up more than I could handle, so I laid my phone on my lap and gazed out the window. A hospital associate drove by on his golf cart, ready to pick up those in need of a quick lift to the entrance.

It struck me as strange that Tracy would repeat her grandfather's words of "an eye for an eye," but I wasn't sure I bought into her believing them for herself. "And if we want to talk about strange," I said to Sweet Pea, snoring in the backseat, "all I have to do is look on Worth

Avenue lately." Things going missing, stolen, then returned. Dead Dominique. Sticky fingers.

I pulled out my phone and resumed my research on the different types of theft.

Burglary, robbery, theft, criminal mischief. "Good old criminal mischief," I said out loud.

A text notification beeped in from Bethany: Someone stole a watercolor off the desk in my backroom while I was up front with a customer.

I texted back: Back door unlocked?

Bethany texted: Not ANYMORE!

Snippy, even via text.

Her next text: Hope they return it. The artist is going to kill me.

Bethany's theft was more than unsettling. It meant the person wasn't going to stop anytime soon, and I truly couldn't leave Sweet Pea alone in Confections ... EVER. It also meant none of us were safe.

I typed into Google's search engine, "Why do people steal and return items?" and one of website links on kleptomania popped up on the screen like popcorn. Kleptomaniacs are ruled by different emotions. Stress can bring on the need to take something, but they often return the items.

"Who has been acting nervous?" I asked my empty front seat.

And how can I catch them in the act?

CHAPTER THIRTY-ONE

I found an interesting blog by a neurologist on how changes in the brain can cause kleptomania. I jumped out of my seat when my cell rang. A number I didn't recognize popped up.

"Is this Miss Armstrong?" the man at the other end of my cell asked.

"Yes?"

"Your friend wants me to tell you she's getting admitted into the hospital."

"Is she going to be alright?"

"This is the best place for her right now," he said in a non-answer.

"Why didn't she call me herself?"

"She's getting tests. You can call later and ask for her room number."

We hung up. Sweet Pea climbed up to the front seat. I opened the passenger window for her and gazed out the windshield. My heart pounded and so did my head. With no time to waste, I called the women on Worth and drove back to Confections.

For the rest of the afternoon, my mind leapt back to Tracy. Every time I called to find her room, the hospital informed me that that she was in the middle of another test. By the time six o'clock rolled around, my insides felt like a cat on a hot tin roof.

Bethany and Jenny came over to Confections with a couple bottles of wine from Bethany's mini-fridge that she kept for prospective purchasers. Even Bethany set aside her snark, worried about our girl Tracy. Snapping Sweet Pea's leash on her now that I couldn't leave her alone even for a minute, I grabbed my purse and the four of us marched across Worth Avenue to Mystic Dreams.

Angelina jumped when the bell above the door clanged. She dropped the watering can she had been holding.

"What are you guys doing here?" she asked, smiling politely.

I let Sweet Pea off her leash. She stuck her snout in a ceramic holder with incense smoke flying upward, and sneezed.

Bethany and Jenny waved the bottles of wine in the air while I set my purse on a center table.

"You're closed, right?" I asked.

Angelina's dress flew behind her as she scurried to the front door and locked it. "Yes, the shop is closed. But it's autumn. We should have apple cider."

"Not unless it's spiked," Bethany said. "The hospital won't let us in to see Tracy, so we thought we could all use a glass of wine to calm ourselves down."

Angelina said, "I have some herbal tea ..." and started to sashay to the back room.

"No!" I said. "It's a glass of wine sort of evening, don't you think?" My tone felt forced, even to my own ears.

Angelina shrugged, and Jenny and Bethany pulled up a few chairs in a casual circle.

Bethany made herself in sole charge of pouring the wine into the glasses she had brought from her art gallery. The five of us sat for a few minutes bemoaning the *ghost fans* situation and wondering how long it would take for customers to return to our businesses for the products instead of the lurid murder details.

I thought Bethany's attempts at humor while we talked sounded as fake as my own, but who was I to judge? After she poured a third glass of wine for all of us, I excused myself to go to the restroom in Mystic Dream's back room. "Back here, right?" I asked Angelina.

She pointed but didn't get up from her chair. "Yes. How many glasses did we have?"

Bethany laughed while I moseyed to the back room, Sweet Pea at my feet.

"Jenny, come help me unzip this stupid zipper, would you please?" I asked, slurring my words a little.

Jenny chuckled and followed me and Sweet Pea.

Bethany said, "I'm going to run to the gallery for crackers so we don't get sick to our stomachs."

"A little late for that," Angelina said and pressed the palm of her hand to her belly.

I zipped in and out of the restroom in record time. Before returning to the main room where Angelina stood alone, I waited at the threshold between front and back. Jenny stood behind me, Sweet Pea at our feet.

The filmy material separating the two sections of the store swayed slightly in the breeze from the overhead fan. I hid myself behind the material and observed Angelina out of the corner of my eye. My purse sat right there on the table. "Think she'll take it?" I whispered to Jenny.

"That's what we're here to find out," she answered quietly.

Angelina turned on music and began dancing.

Two minutes later, Bethany swept through the front door holding an open box of crackers and said loudly to Angelina, "I got hungry on the way over. Did that wine hit you like it did me?"

Angelina fished into the box and crammed the rest of the crackers into her mouth, then waved her arms in a drunken sway and twirled, almost knocking a gold Buddha off his plush, velvet cushion.

I whispered to Jenny. "Okay, your turn. Since she didn't steal my purse, next up is to see if you can get her talking."

"You're not coming out with me?"

"No. The fewer of us, the more chance she'll open up."

Jenny fell sideways into me but righted herself as best she could. "Like we planned, right?" she asked, her voice thick from the alcohol.

"Yup," I said and smiled reassuringly.

Jenny wobbled out to the front where Angelina chewed crackers and danced, and Bethany busied herself at a table full of miniature Buddhas.

"Angelina," Jenny said. "Who are those two people that keep coming by?"

Angelina tensed for a moment. "No one important."

"Come *on*," Jenny whined.

Behind the filmy curtain, I held Sweet Pea's head close to my thigh.

"Alright, I'll tell you," Angelina said. "But if I tell you, you have to tell me something."

"Okay," Jenny said. "What?"

"I'll ask you after I tell you about them. Do you promise?"

Jenny nodded while Bethany fell into an incense rack and knocked it over, then giggled.

Angelina tried righting the rack but her hands slipped and it crashed to the ground. Sweet Pea grew restless at my heels. I reached down and massaged her ears.

Tittering, Angelina wobbled from side to side and dropped into a chair. "Oh, they're a couple of people I know from back home."

"In Ocala?" Jenny asked.

"Yes. I went to school with them. They sort of tortured me through the years. I didn't dress like the others and I always liked magic."

"So what are they doing here?" Jenny asked and smiled at Bethany topping her wine glass to the tippy-top.

"They heard I work at a New Age store and can't help themselves from giving me a hard time about it."

"Is that true?" Jenny sat down next to the shop manager and almost fell over in her chair.

Angelina laughed and play-hit her on the arm. "You're drunk!"

Jenny play-hit her back, only harder.

"Hey!" said Angelina and rubbed her arm. She straightened in her seat and ran a hand across her face, smearing her lipstick. Everything was going as planned. "Alright, I told you. Now you tell me. You poisoned Dominique because she caught you stealing, and then you killed her when she was proving to be too much of a threat, right?"

My heart pounded like a bass drum.

Jenny's eyes shot up to Angelina and Bethany, but her mouth remained closed.

"Oh, come on," said Angelina, "it's not like we'll remember in the morning."

Jenny chortled. "You're drunk."

My flowery friend drew herself up out of her chair and began pacing back and forth. She broke out in sobs and admitted, "It's not kids from school. It's my brother and sister. They won't leave me alone."

Astonished, I held my breath.

Angelina turned to the gold clock sitting on a rosewood table. "They'll probably be coming soon. They come here almost the same time every evening and sometimes in the mornings, too. I don't know what to do!"

Sweet Pea and I joined them in the front of the shop. Angelina stumbled, and from all appearances, appeared like she would fall and crack her head open on a marble table.

"What do they want from you?" I asked, truly surprised at this turn of events.

"My parents own an auto parts store. We were told to always keep it in the family. Compete against the big stores, not go down without a fight."

Bethany chuckled. "An auto parts store? You?"

Angelina ran a hand across her face in a drunken gesture.

Jenny said, "Just tell them you have a new life and to leave you alone." She swiped at her face. Drool ran out the corner of her mouth.

"It's not that easy," Angelina said. "We were raised that we were to continue our parents' business. It's ingrained."

"Well, un-grain it, then," said Bethany.

"It's easy for all of you. I don't have anyone. We had no neighbors and no friends because I was too busy working at the store every day after school and on weekends."

"That was a long time ago," Bethany offered. "You're a grown woman now."

"I said it's not that simple!" Angelina said in a loud, drunken voice.

"We're here for you," I said quietly. "Whatever you need."

Jenny and Bethany nodded. We all gulped from our wine glasses. My plan had been thrown a curve ball, but it didn't mean all was lost.

Bethany focused the conversation back to our point in being there. "If we could find out who is stealing and who killed Dominique, I think we would all feel better."

Angelina nodded.

Jenny smiled at me. I encouraged her with a nod to press on.

She turned to Angelina and slurred, "You can tell us ... you're the one who has been stealing, right? It makes you feel in control, powerful?"

All our eyes gazed upon Angelina, who dropped her jaw in horror.

"Me? No ..."

"It's okay," I said. "Kleptomaniacs just have a little bit of a brain warp. It's nothing to be ashamed of."

Jenny added, "Unless *you're* the one who killed Dominique, which makes you a murderer. Oh my God. Are you?"

"If you all think it was me who killed Dominique, why don't you get proof?" Angelina shouted, very unlike her. "I dare you!" She held on to the corner of a table, then stumbled to the back of the store.

Bethany and Jenny, never shying away from a dare, caught my eye.

"Well, that wasn't very nice of us, accusing her of killing Dominique," I said, feeling my lips move in strange directions as I slurred. "And it didn't even do any good. So much for being plastered and sharing all our darkest secrets."

Bethany shrugged. "It's nice to feel like I'm back in college with a bunch of girlfriends, telling each other things. I miss those days." Her eyelids closed sleepily.

A smile crept onto Jenny's lips. She leaned over, almost falling over her own lap when her elbow missed her knee. "Samantha, when we ran into each other in front of my doctor's office, I sort of fibbed." *Fibbed* came out *vibbed*. "I wasn't seeing the doctor to deal with Dominique's murder," she explained. "I was seeing the doctor way before that."

I lifted my eyebrows at her.

She nodded. "My brain hasn't been the same since the surfing accident." She leaned back in her chair and laughed, spittle streaming out of the corner of her mouth.

Angelina returned from the back, still stumbling but with a dry face.

"We'll help you with your brother and sister," I said to her. "We've got your back."

"Thank you." She turned to Bethany. "Do you mind if we get some more crackers from Bebe? I'm still feeling nauseous from all of that wine."

"Sure," Bethany replied.

The two women staggered to the front door, opened it, and strode arm in arm across Worth Avenue.

I grabbed Sweet Pea's leash and said to Jenny, "I'll be right back. I'm just going to run over to Confections for some apple cider after all. Angelina is right. It's autumn. We should make the most of the season."

Jenny held her glass of wine and swayed in her chair with half-closed eyes to Yanni's piano music wafting from Angelina's speakers.

I held Sweet Pea's leash in front of Mystic Dreams, watched Bethany and Angelina disappear inside Gallery Bebe, and glanced behind me at Jenny swaying to the beat in a wine stupor.

Sweet Pea and I darted around the Mystic Dreams building. The wide alleyways were empty. We came upon Mystic Dreams' patio. I held my ear up to the back door. Nothing. I opened the door slowly, entered the back room, and stopped at the same filmy material between front and back where Jenny and I had been standing a few minutes ago.

I pulled my cell phone from my pocket, turned the video on, directed it to the front room, and waited for the action to begin. Bethany and Angelina were due to arrive back at any moment. Alone in the front of the shop, Jenny laid a green apple on a shelf. A manchineel apple like I had seen on the Travel Channel, I was sure of it. I looked at my cell and confirmed that the red record button was on. Next, I marveled at Jenny angling the fruit so that it would be obvious but not so obvious that it looked like it had been planted. *No one ever accused her of being a dummy.*

Angelina marched through the front door by herself. Jenny wheeled around to face her.

No longer stumbling, Angelina strode over to Jenny. "What's that?"

I checked the record button again, clear of head and steady of hand, thankful the second of the two bottles of wine Bethany had brought over to serve all of us except Jenny was non-alcoholic.

Jenny slurred, "What's it look like?"

Angelina said with perfect clarity and none of the slur from a few minutes ago, "I think it looks like you're the one who poisoned and then killed Dominique, and you want to make it look like it was me."

"Well, aren't you a brain full of smarts? You think I was going to let Dominique go around telling everyone I was the thief? Kleptomania is a mental illness." She swiped at the spittle streaming from her mouth.

"And murder?" Angelina asked. "What's your excuse for that?"

"That's me protecting myself from getting found out and sent back to the mental hospital they put me in after my surfing accident. One little murder threat to the owner of the surfing company, and they throw me in a hospital. Does that seem fair to you?" She reached out for Angelina's hair, missed, and fell on the floor.

Sweet Pea whimpered at my side behind the curtain. I held her back, not only to keep her from the fray, but also to keep her from interrupting my plan with Bethany and Angelina to get it all on video.

"Are you okay?" Angelina asked Jenny, sprawled on the floor with her hair draped across her face. "You didn't hit your head again, did you?"

Angelina leaned over to check on Jenny, who pulled the New Age shopkeeper down to the ground with her. Their subsequent brawl was less brutish and more comedy-hour, thanks to Jenny being plastered and missing every shot at Angelina's face.

I held my cell phone steadily with one hand to get the entire thing on tape for the police. My other hand gripped Sweet Pea's leash.

Jenny huffed and breathed heavily from the floor. "There's no way my friends are going to blame me for killing Dominique, you fragile little creature." She stood up, stumbled, and spat, "*I'm* the thief, *I'm* the murderer, but who is going to believe that with a loony-tune like *you* around?"

"Me," I said and marched out to the front room, Sweet Pea at my side.

Bethany flung the front door open. "And me."

I held my cell in the air. "And oh, anyone who gets hold of this video with your full confession."

Bethany and Angelina, completely sober, surrounded Jenny.

"Thanks to Samantha's research skills and impatience," Bethany said, "we had a feeling it was you wreaking havoc on our strip of Worth Avenue."

The front door flew open again. Because this was part of the plan to solve two problems at one time, my insides danced with glee that everything was falling into place. Though at the time of the plan Angelina had confided she was truly at the end of her rope due to the two unwanted visitors, I didn't know they were her siblings. Now, as her brother and sister entered the store, we would help her out of this mess once and for all.

"Agnes, I don't know who all of these people are and I don't care. Enough is enough," her brother said with a firm voice.

Bethany whispered into my ear, "Agnes?"

"Shhh," I whispered back.

Angelina's sister joined her brother in the onslaught. "We keep telling you … you need to come home, and we're here to take you."

"I'm not coming," Angelina said.

The sister explained to us, "I don't know who you all are, but Agnes ran away from home fourteen years ago when she was fifteen. But our father isn't well. He can't run the store anymore." To Angelina, "You're coming with us."

"No," Angelina said again.

I spread my arms in front of her. "I agree. No."

From behind me, someone pulled my hair, hard. Sweet Pea barked one time.

I reached up to grab the hand holding a wad of my hair and tried to turn, but it hurt too much. I finally inched my head around enough to see Jenny, wildly drunk and grinning.

"Ow!" I shouted when she wouldn't let go.

Sweet Pea barked sharply again at Jenny, who released her grasp on my hair.

My furry dog panted loudly and didn't take her eyes off of us.

Jenny, reeking of red wine, shrieked and tried to fling herself on top of me but missed. Sweet Pea lunged on top of her. All thirty-five pounds. Which doesn't sound like a lot of weight unless you're blitzed on red wine and prescription drugs. The pastry shop manager fell to the ground. Sweet Pea didn't bite her, only laid on top of her and panted.

The rest of us—me, Bethany, Angelina, and Angelina's brother and sister—gaped at the sight of my sweet dog on top of the slight woman.

Sensing her hero status, Sweet Pea lay with legs splayed and tail tentatively wagging while Jenny below her lay like a sleepy infant with a belly full of baby formula.

Somebody—I don't remember who—called 911, and I guided Sweet Pea off of Jenny, to protect my dog more than the woman ... I didn't trust the Patisserie manager not to fling her off.

Bethany said to Angelina's siblings, "You two can leave now. And you know not to come back, right?"

They looked at each other, then at Angelina.

Head lifted, shoulders raised in a stance I hadn't seen on the woman before, Angelina said, "I'll visit with Dad and help with what I can, but I'm not moving back, and I'm not going to be bullied by you anymore."

Surprised looks crossed the siblings' faces. Their gaze moved from Angelina to me to Bethany and back to Angelina. Finally, they looked at each other and, seeming to sense it was no use, left the shop. I breathed a sigh of relief and waited with the others for the police to arrive and arrest Jenny.

While we waited, Angelina said, "My sister and brother were making me more and more nervous. It's hard to believe family can still have that effect on you, even when you're all grown up."

"Don't I know it," Jenny said with a slur from the floor.

Bethany said to Jenny, "Except your parents and psychiatrist wanted you in a mental hospital, and Agnes's family were only trying to guilt her into coming home to run the family business."

Angelina stepped over and said quietly into Bethany's ear, "It's still Angelina."

Before Bethany could return Angelina's polite request with something snarky, I said, "If your brother and sister try it again, you need to keep us in the loop and not think you have to be a hero, alright?"

"Sweet Pea is the hero here," she said with a smile.

I beamed at my furry baby.

"And anyway," Angelina said, "I wasn't trying to be a hero. I was embarrassed. But all of this was worth it, catching the thief and Dominique's murderer, all rolled into one woman." She nodded down at Jenny. "I knew my high school drama class would come in handy one day."

I said to Bethany, "Angelina's acting was good but yours? Not so much."

Bethany said, "Like you're Meryl Streep?"

Jenny, the only one who was drunk, tried to stand up but instead slumped back to the floor next to the table with the green apple lookalike.

Bethany confirmed, "That's a manchineel apple, then?"

I nodded. "Yup."

"If the fruit does everything you said," said Angelina, "it's pretty frightening."

"In the wrong hands, it is," I replied.

Jenny lifted her head and said accusingly, "You said we were going to force a confession from Angelina." Her mouth twisted from the alcohol so that *Angelina* came out *Anewina*.

"That's what you were supposed to think," I responded.

"You *ticked* me."

Bethany said smugly, "You deserve it after going along with Samantha's pretend plan to frame Angelina."

"And for killing Dominique, by the way," I said pointedly to Bethany.

"That too," Bethany replied. "We didn't get much time to talk this charade through when you called earlier today. "You learned about the manchineel apple and kleptomania on the Travel Channel?"

I nodded and petted Sweet Pea. "At first, yeah. I found out the rest online. It's amazing what you can learn by clicking the right links."

"How did Jenny not get blisters and stomach issues by messing with those apples?" Bethany asked.

"Haven't you ever noticed the box of gloves on her counter?" I turned to Angelina. "For a while, I thought the lack of fingerprints might be from you, always wearing different kinds of gloves. Come to find out, you're just stylish."

Jenny sat up for a second and vomited. Bethany and Angelina grimaced.

"She does that," I said.

"Is she okay?" Angelina asked.

"She'll be fine. The same thing happened when she drank a Margarita." I peered over at the girl who couldn't hold her liquor. "It's a good thing I found out what a lightweight you are. It came in very handy for my purposes here tonight." The wheels in my mind spun. Placing my attention on Bethany and Angelina, I explained, "She retaliated against anyone who went against her—Dominique, for insisting she would find the thief. Tracy, for saying whoever killed Dominique deserves what's coming to them ..."

Blisters! Tracy!

"I almost forgot about Tracy!" I checked my phone. "Geez, I really need to remember to turn my text notifications on."

A text from Tracy: Looks like a reaction to some kind of poisonous fruit. I'm okay.

I swung around to Jenny, wiping her mouth with the back of her hand. "You put some of that green apple on Tracy's espresso cup at Confections, didn't you," I said as a statement rather than a question. "And somehow snuck wearing gloves while you did it."

"I *knew* it was strange that she'd carry a big handbag like that. Since when is she fashionable?" said Bethany.

Jenny, too sloshed from the wine and sick from the nausea to put up a fight, simply shrugged and plunked her head to the ground.

I pressed my lips together and rejoiced that Tracy would be okay. Turning my attention away from the murderer on the floor and toward my friends, I announced, "Tracy is going to be fine."

Everyone whooped. Sweet Pea danced around us.

"I want to go to the hospital to see her," I said. "Think Trumble will mind if I leave you with my video?"

The front door flew open. Rick and the woman I had seen him with on multiple occasions strode inside. He grinned. "I keep seeing people come in and out over here. Thought we would crash your party."

I tried for a 100-watt smile, but I'm pretty sure it only came at about 70.

"And I wanted to introduce you to ..." Rick's eyes fell to Jenny on the floor. "What's up with her?"

"Agnes is throwing a wild party," snarked Bethany.

I ribbed her with my elbow and whispered, "Shush."

Angelina said, "We'll fill you in later." She glanced at me and smiled that lovely smile, then reached out gracefully to the woman next to Rick. "Hi. I'm Angelina."

Traitor, I thought and laughed to myself. I would probably befriend Rick's new girlfriend too, no matter how much I preferred to be in her place.

Rick ran a hand through his thick hair. "This is my sister, Teresa. She's been visiting from the West Coast of Florida."

Sister. I started over to her but stopped when Mystic Dreams' front door flew open yet again, this time with Trumble and his team.

The detective took one look at Jenny on the floor and shook his head at me. "The next time I catch you infiltrating my murder case on Worth Avenue, you're going to find yourself in trouble."

I didn't know what bothered me more. Trumble's threat that next time I'd be in trouble ...

... or the fact that he thought there was going to be another murder on Worth Avenue.

THE END

Cheese Please Hound Rounds

*Another recipe from Chef Sarah Deters at the test kitchen
of Three Dog Bakery, the original bakery for dogs!*

Bakes up approximately 24 chewy, cheesy chompers

2 cups white flour

½ cup shredded low-fat Cheddar cheese

½ cup low-fat cottage cheese

1 tsp chopped cilantro leaves

1 tsp parsley flakes

2 TBSP vegetable oil

¾ cup chopped peanuts

2/3 cup water

- Preheat oven to 375.
- Mix together flour, Cheddar and cottage cheese, cilantro leaves and parsley.
- Add oil, peanuts and water and mix thoroughly.
- Break off golf ball-size pieces and shape into balls.
- Place on greased baking sheet and bake for 30 minutes. Cool on a rack and serve. Store in a sealed container if the refrigerator.

Coming Soon!

Book 3 in the Canine Confections Mystery Series

PAWS FOR DEATH

Made in the USA
Las Vegas, NV
11 September 2021